Dedicat[illegible]

Dedicated to Mary, Christine and Carissa.

Saul of Solway

An account of his wanderings.

*

James Bovill

PART ONE

1

I knew this guy, Saul. Pal of mine; bit of a gallant. Would see him at irregular intervals, because he never stayed in one place. He loved to go to meetings, and would travel around lots of the towns and cities in central Scotland.

He came originally from some small place on the southwest coast, but his whole adult life had been spent in the city. He liked to say that he was a creature from the sea, who had learned to grow legs and run. Dunno really what he meant by all that; it was just sort of the way he talked. He loved to talk. And he loved to listen.

Maybe listening to other people talking was one of the reasons he liked going to meetings: local golf club closure protest meetings; allotment meetings; A.A. meetings; Celtic Supporters Club meetings; pub darts team meetings; bowling club meetings; local government election meetings; religious minorities' rights meetings; Association of Pipers meetings… He just loved them, and attended as many as he could.

A problem arose when he accrued twelve points on his driving licence and was banned from driving for a year. He had been speeding, trying to make it to a West of Scotland Druids meeting, down in Oban, and was running late. This was a terrible blow to a man who loved (and needed) to get to his meetings nearly every day. He lay quiet for a while; I never saw him for months.

Then I heard what happened next – you might not believe this, but you would if you knew the guy. His pal's uncle owned a farm, and Saul had spent a few summer holidays there, where he had learned how to ride a horse. Now, after about five weeks without a meeting, he was going crazy, so he hired a horse from a friend, (who was also a bookie, funnily enough), along with all the necessary accoutrements, and started riding to meetings. A long time later he showed me the notebook the bookie had given him, along with the horse, containing page after page of strict and precise instructions for all eventualities. Saul had memorized most of the contents – he had obviously taken very seriously this opportunity to travel by horse; along with all of his weaknesses, in certain respects he had an iron discipline.

For many meetings, there is adjacent car parking nearby, for use by the members. But not even the Orange Lodge provided stabling facilities for horses of visiting cowboys! And, looping a horse's reins around a post isn't as easy as the cowboys used to make it look. Still, Saul insisted the plan would work until he got his licence back.

But it was not to be. How that all came around is a separate story, but I can give you a summary version of it here.

The horse was called Trigger, perhaps as a tribute to the stallion Roy Rogers brought to Glasgow's Empire Pavilion, in 1954. Together, they managed to get to the first two meetings, which were both quite close at hand. The first – a Dairy Lads A.G.M., near East Kilbride – was held in a barn, and Trigger was tethered peaceably enough, in a little wood nearby.

The second meeting, a little farther off, in Bridge of Allen, was more difficult. This was a Robert Burns Appreciation Society get-together, and it involved a formal meal, so it was held in a restaurant, bang in the middle of town – with nowhere to tie a horse! They came to an agreement that, if Saul stayed outside with Trigger, right beside one of the windows, they would open the window and Saul could participate in the meeting, while keeping hold of the horse's reins at the same time. It was not ideal – far from it – but enough to satisfy the crazy Saul, and prevent him from exploding into a rampage. Some of the Burns members had once before witnessed Saul in a rampage and didn't ever want to see it again. Later that week, Saul received a letter making it clear that neither he nor his steed would be welcome back.

The third outing (and the final one, as it turned out) was to a meeting held monthly in Dumbarton, by the Sons of The Rock: some weird Celtic cult who treated the Clyde like a sacred river, and all that sort of stuff. For this meeting, participants had to wear a special uniform, including knee-high boots with high heels. And these may have played a key part in Saul's downfall – for a downfall it was… literally! Galloping along (late as usual) by Bowling and Old Kilpatrick, with Dumbarton now in his sights, Saul was blinded by the light of the setting sun, as he came around a bend; Trigger swerved to avoid the tree Saul was steering them right at, and Saul went a-tumbling.

Concussed and bruised, but otherwise uninjured, he came to in a small copse of trees, just below the A82. His head continued to swim for a while, then he pulled himself to his feet and scrambled up the bank, to the roadside verge. He started walking. When he realized he was heading back toward Glasgow, he turned and made for Dumbarton.

Within a few minutes, he fainted and fell – almost right into the path of a Honda Jazz. The car stopped and its driver rushed to see how he was. Strangely, the woman showed no reaction to his dark green (with silver ribbing), high-heeled, soft kid-leather, knee-length boots. Saul recalled that the dialogue went roughly as follows:

"Are you okay? What happened? Where are you going?"

"Where's my horse? Where's Trigger? I have to go back..." He pushed himself to his feet, but staggered, and had to steady himself against the bonnet of the Honda. He saw the woman looking at him, and realized he appeared a lost musketeer in the wrong land. He tried to brush off some of the mud which had smeared onto his right boot.

"I have a horse – a bay horse, nine years old, brought me here; I came off him, just at that bend. He should be around here somewhere. I know, I know... it's a long story: no driving licence; many places to visit... meetings... meetings all over the place. You ever hear of the Sons of the Rock?"

"Are they a band? A group, I mean. Music?"

"No, they're an organization; a company of people who believe in certain things about Dumbarton, about the Clyde. The main man is Pierre; he's the First Son, although it's funny that his name is sort of French. I have his number here somewhere. Could you phone him for me? Sorry, I'm seeing double right now. Thanks for helping. What's your name?"

"Corinthia. Let's have your phone."

"Wow! Corinthia – that's a cracker of a name! Oh, sorry; look for Pierre in the contacts."

They had no luck getting through – probably because the meeting was already starting, and old Pierre would be too busy for phone calls. Who knew what might be rising up outa the Clyde? The Sons of the Rock had to be vigilant!

Saul said: "Right, Corinthia, I'll have to speak to my pal Zeke; see if he'll come and bail me out. You'll find him under *'Z'*: Z for Zeke. Zeke is a trusty pal; he's like the brother I never had. I'm Saul, by the way."

She dialled Zeke, but he refused to come and help. He said that he liked Saul's company, but Saul was a psycho, and Zeke's family had made him solemnly promise not to go anywhere near him.

So, she said: "I'm taking you along to the Dumbarton Cottage Hospital, where they can check that you're okay; you still don't look right. Then I'll take you where you need to go, so long as it's not too far."

She took his arm, to help him into the Honda. As she did so, she admired a striking tattoo on the inside of his left wrist: a short sword or maybe a dagger, standing out more startlingly than most tattoos, which tend to be dull.

At the hospital, he was found to have mild concussion but allowed to go home. She took him back to Glasgow and dropped him off.

Two nights later, on a night out with her pals, she heard herself saying: "You'll never guess what happened to me."

Saul went into a lengthy gloom, most unlike him. He was forced to face the facts: his days of roving, and nights of meetings, were coming to an end. And now the bookie had phoned, looking for his horse back. Saul tried to explain that the animal had gone missing.

"First Shergar," said the bookie, "now Trigger."

Saul's escape from the bookie is another story, and I don't have time for it just now.

I thought then that I knew Saul quite well, but that was all to change, though only after a series of events got unpacked.

I have never been one for meetings myself, and tend to stay away from them; too boring, usually held up some rickety stairs, in some garret with creaking boards and an atmospheric skylight. Some people go to meetings just looking for a fight, yet many go to enjoy some companionship, under whatever particular banner the meeting is held. Apart from that, you don't know what to expect. You would think that a bakery meeting would be duller than a political meeting, but not necessarily.

Saul once took me along with him to a meeting; said he needed a minder. It was over in Carntyne. I drove him across the city, and on the way he regaled me with some of his history:

"Just after our fifth year in school, I found a way to at last get out of The Home: I got a girlfriend called Teresa. She was quite keen on me, but more than that she felt sorry for me. She told her mum about me – an orphan with nowhere to stay – and her mother took me in. I was given a room, and it was made clear that there was to be no traffic between bedrooms; I don't think she was all that serious, but we tried to keep to the rules. After all, Catherine (Teresa's mother) was doing me a big favour.

"Catherine was in voluntary social work, where she was some sort of coordinator, and a great many meetings were held at her spacious house. Sometimes there would be local councillors present, sometimes prospective candidates, and other people working at different levels throughout the social services. Sometimes, if she was under pressure, Catherine would ask me to help, as a waiter to the guests, bringing coffee, tea or juice and biscuits. Often I hung around, and managed to pick up a fair amount of the jargon and patois of the meetings.

"I came to like being at the meetings. I liked the formalities especially, of which there was variety but also regularity: a chairperson, treasurer, secretary and specific rules for the conduct of the meeting. The meeting essentials impressed me then; they were needed to help our long journey, learning how to get along with one another – that sort of progress only came about through meetings.

"A few years later, when Teresa and I had gone our separate ways, and I got my own place, I used a lot of my spare time going to meetings. I would look out for notices and posters – the crazier the better – and pop up in Clydebank or Motherwell, as the kind of token spirit of the meeting. My presence at some meetings was questioned, especially at first; I might be asked what my interest was in the frequency of bin collections in Yoker, and so on. Gradually, though, I was accepted just about everywhere."

I had my doubts about Saul's explanation. Especially later, when I discovered that there could be other reasons for his meeting-mania. To be honest, trying to keep this story of Saul in line is already proving tricky.

Anyway, at this Carntyne meeting I noticed that Saul was careful to take a look at everybody present, though not in an intrusive way; for all his declared fascination with proceedings, he seemed more interested in the people present. The main business had been the proposed shutdown of a local municipal golf course. I had never heard Saul mention golf before, but he seemed to enjoy watching it, when it was shown onscreen at The Palace.

On the way back home from Carntyne, I asked Saul if he was happy with how the meeting went, and how it rated as a meeting in his estimation. He was surprisingly vocal:

"For a start, how can a fat man called Bailey become a Baillie?! It's just nuts; it's bringing mockery into the whole proceedings! That fat guy strutted up and down there like some old pharaoh, with the fate of thousands in his hand, pontificating about the golf courses of his youth. What a liar! Never played golf in his life – as I happened to find out. Believe me, that cause is lost; from next year there'll be no golf played at Victoria Park – maybe there won't even *be* a Victoria Park. He just played for time – the sanctimonious old git – with all that stuff about, 'I promise you from my heart of hearts,' and 'I will never rest until I get to the bottom of this.'

"A lot of people made their feelings really clear; there was some real anger in there – but it's all too late. Still, I said my piece, and I said it well. We got the promise of a follow-up meeting in four months, but the deal will be done by then! And the men behind the scenes – those cloak-and-dagger villains who have always plagued Glasgow's city council – will be happy. They'll be relieved they got away with grand larceny… and they'll be a lot richer. But, before you ask, if there is a follow-up meeting I'll be there."

There was some conviction in all of this. But something was odd: Saul claimed that he had said his piece at the meeting, and said it well; he gave an impression of doing all he could for them. But he seemed to forget that I hadn't left the room, and I knew that, although Saul had muttered a few brief observations to me and the chap on his other side, he made no actual contribution to the debate. He never spoke a word.

2

I had seen Saul drink in The Palace of Mirrors many times before. Even if he disappeared for a few weeks, nobody had any doubts that he would be back.

Whatever trade he did was unknown, though most regulars knew that he played the bagpipes and depended a lot on gigs for income. He was never short of money, though he did not flash it around, never appeared overdressed, or talked about the latest technology or furniture he had bought; his car was a little Nissan, neat and reliable. He just had no appetite for looking well off or showy.

It was well known that he loved The Palace, like many of us. He was a regular irregular – as was his demeanour; his was blood where the mercury ran free. One night he would buy you a double; another night he would insist on selling you a crockery set or a D.V.D. player. So, it was something of a surprise when he said to me, one Tuesday night, that he had to go to an A.A. meeting, and asked would I like to come along. I had been an attendee at A.A. many years before, and maybe Saul had got to hear of that; he had a wonderful network buzzing for him. The pint of Kronenbourg he was drinking obviously did not fit well with this request, so I was intrigued and agreed to come along. Of course, I had a couple of questions.

"Let's sit down," he said (we always stood at the bar). "Go ahead."

"A.A., Saul? I don't think you can just walk in there unless... well, unless you want to stop drinking."

"We've both tried A.A., long ago, but surely you remember that there are closed meetings and there are open meetings, and anybody is free to sit in on an open meeting."

"Yes, but... why would you want to? Are you quitting the booze? Is it to be Saul's life-changing moment?"

"You remember Becky McMillan?"

I nodded.

"I thought you did. Well, she married Craig. Craig has gone to pot; terrible state: money, gangs, drink, dope, terrible company, jobs lost... the whole works. Especially drink. Well, I met Becky outa the blue last week, and she said that Craig was desperate to change, but he was terrified. He wanted off the drink, and thought that A.A. might help him, but he was scared stiff of going. I mentioned that I knew of an A.A. meeting held on Thursdays, at Hogganfield. I said to Becky that I would go with him as support, if he really wanted to go. She was really chuffed, and said that she would see what he said. Then, on Sunday, Craig phones me to take up my offer. So, I'm picking him up at 7.45; meeting starts at eight."

"Does he live in Hogganfield?"

"Don't know; he wouldn't tell me where he lived. Said he would meet me at the venue, across the street from an off-licence. Said there was always plenty of space for parking."

"What about Becky?"

"What about Becky?"

"Will she be there?"

"Ah, just as I thought! I knew you would take the bait! You did fancy her a lot, didn't you, way back when?"

"I think I loved Becky once. I suppose she wouldn't have been that difficult to find – now and then her name would come up – but I can get very lazy about things, even important things."

But this story is about Saul…

That same night, at nine p.m., he said: "Right, that's me; I'm off." And he left the pub.

Incredible. Offering to help a treacherous wastrel: incredible! Going to a meeting of Alcoholics Anonymous…? Incredible.

I'd just settled down to read *The Times*, when Saul burst back in and sat down.

"I've just remembered, my pal Zeke once tried his luck with Becky and got totally rebuffed. Just think, Becky rejects Zeke, the best of the lot of us, and lands up with Craig! That's women for you: beyond understanding. So, if you're thinking too far ahead, just remember I warned you. My cousin Tommy was another who fancied his chances with her; Becky turned him into some sort of paté."

I'd forgotten about Tom. Very much a man who preferred the shadows to the light, but an enigma as well. Surely a far bigger catch than the Craig she had tied herself to. I hadn't forgotten about Becky, but I was too battle-scarred nowadays for a new campaign.

"Anyway, come along. You'll be helping Becky, and that'll be good. Just watch what you say in front of Craig, mind; he's a little unbalanced."

Then, he was finally gone.

The Thursday meeting was "open", but in every other detail proceeded along the format of all A.A. meetings. There was a top table, with a chairwoman and a guest speaker; there was a big rectangular arrangement of desks with seats; there were tea, coffee and biscuits to greet you, along with hearty handshakes and cordial wishes expressed.

At eight sharp, a bell rang and we took our seats. Men outnumbered women by seven to three. Somehow, Craig got shunted along the side opposite to us, so I was beside Saul, looking straight across at him. He did a fair amount of twitching and blinking – who knew whether or not that was a good sign?

The meeting finished at nine-thirty, with a full-voiced rendering of the *Serenity Prayer*. Afterward, we stood in the car park, while Craig had a smoke. When Saul recognized somebody and went over to say hello, I tried to draw Craig into a conversation. I really wanted to ask him about Becky – but how could I? So, I tried a more obvious topic, asking had he enjoyed the meeting, what he had got out of it, and would he be going back?

He had little to say. He was more than elusive, in fact: he was downright shifty, and still twitching. I didn't give much for his chances.

Then, he did reveal a little: "I'm sure I could find a better meeting than that. I don't like sitting in a circle; I get dead nervous. I bet there are meetings where the chairs are in rows, facing the front – that would be my kind of meeting."

"Right, right. Well, there are still a few punters hanging around; why don't you go over and ask one of them?"

He looked horrified, yet to my surprise he said, "Okay," then rolled over to guys by the door. By then, Saul was on his way back. I told him that Craig was making a few enquiries.

"That's a good sign; he's showing some interest. That's great."

"Maybe."

Craig came back, saying that his next meeting would be at St. Simon's Hall in Partick, on Monday. He sounded firm and definite – maybe that was why Saul just nodded, without offering to go with him. Then, Craig squeezed into his car and drove off, without a word of thanks or anything else. Maybe he was troubled. Well, according to Saul's catalogue of Craig's woes, he had a right to be.

Over time, I went to a handful – maybe a few more – of these meetings, and the strangest thing to me was that Saul never spoke. That is, he never contributed in words, though he did a fair amount of nodding, shaking his head, tutting or sometimes applauding. It seemed so odd to travel such distances, sit through meetings and never speak. But he listened intently. I began to think that there was maybe some other programme ticking away in his head, guiding him.

Maybe, I wondered, *he takes notes when he gets home, and compares the meetings, entering all this data into a complex file system? Or maybe it's some academic study – something in sociology, perhaps – and he's planning on releasing some astonishing thesis about meetings in Scotland?* Neither speculation seemed very plausible. Maybe it could just as well be dismissed as an unusual hobby; many hobbies are weird. Still, inside Saul some other motor was turning.

I just kept following, now sort of tangled up in Saul. Okay, maybe that's a little overdramatic.

One night at The Palace, I was in a wee group, and asked if any of them had ever accompanied Saul to any of his meetings. To my surprise, two of the guys knew nothing of the meetings. But The Dodger had been along with him.

"I was at a coupla sessions wi' Saul, coupla year ago. Wan wis in Brigton – some bloody Masonic thing – though obviously no' wan o' their secret meetin's, or ah widda been barred right away; naw, it wis aboot The Lodge's contribution to charities in the Brigton area. Quite interesting, noo that ah remember it. But ah think it was mainly a prefab job, tae get them some positive publicity – sure needed it, efter that rammy at Brigton Cross; two deid. Man, that wis the auld days, back wi' a bang. Apparently, Saul wis there as a delegate fae some sailors' charity, at the Broomielaw; Saul did some voluntary night-work there. So, ah actually expected Saul tae speak, tae contribute, since he had some experience of urban homeless, and all that – don't know aboot sailors, though; Saul's no' a sailor – but the thing is he did not speak throughout the meetin'. Looked fully interested, listened quite seriously and had an opening a coupla times, but stayed silent. Even ah nearly chipped in some ideas masel'! Thought better of it, though. Just as well.

"Then, comin' back from Brigton, Saul wis different: odd, ah mean; kinda nervy and agitated. By the time we got back oot here he was okay. Whole thing left me puzzled.

"I did go to another meetin' wi' him, after that: some kinda comedy production, at a wee theatre over in Rutherglen. Canny mind much aboot it; ah wiz pretty drunk that night, as I recall. But I do remember being happy, because Saul was really enjoying it; really laughing and roaring, looking like he was having a great time. Ye don't get that look affa Saul very often. It wiz an amateur group, and they needed a few places tae fill, for some Gilbert and Sullivan nonsense they wir planning. Saul woulda been perfect for wan o' these small parts, and he widda loved it, but, despite all the enjoyment he wiz showin', when it came tae it, he turned it doon; 'No' fir me,' he said, 'ah'm better oan the ootside.'"

3

Then came the ride to Dumbarton and its sombre consequences. No car, no licence, no horse… and then, in a delayed effect of that fall from Trigger, he had a screwed-up right hip and a limp, which he was warned would be permanent.

Because Gartnaval Hospital, where he was getting his treatment, was less than half a mile away from The Palace of Mirrors, he made The Palace his regular base, calculating that it would be the best hub for getting to his most important meetings. He built up a circle of contacts, and was able to get lifts to places he wanted to attend. He paid guys to rickshaw him around, and bought them drinks. Anyway, I was in The Palace one night, talking – or rather, listening – to Dark Cloud Phil, when he casually remarked that Saul was in hospital. So, the next day I went along to see him.

I expected to find him in Orthopaedics, but he was in a general ward, along with a number of obvious accident victims.

"He's in for his hip, right?" I asked the doctor.

The doctor was puzzled. "Hip? Yes, but mainly ribs, elbow and ankle; also, some scraping to his face. He was struck by a van on Great Western Road; apparently, he just stepped out into its path. People do forget where they are. I spoke to him a little, but I can't say I understood what must have happened."

A few visitors had been in, but none of them had come away any the wiser. Saul was a livewire, yes, and a bit reckless, yes, but a suicide? Surely never.

"John!" Saul said, with a relief which surprised me. I had known him on and off for years, but you could not say we were buddies. Yet, the look on his face said relief and delight.

Maybe he's badly concussed, I thought, *and he's mistaken me for somebody else?*

As soon as they pulled over the privacy curtain, the delight and relief fell away. "John, I've been waiting for you. You feeling okay just now? Good, cos I have something to tell you, and I think I need your help. I think I might be on the verge of something! Remember that Eagles line, *'this could be Heaven or this could be Hell'*? It's a bit like that, John; exciting, maybe mystical, but it chilled me to the bone! Are you following me?"

There was no answer to that. His relief had changed to anxiety, and it was earnest and deep – quite different from anything I'd seen in Saul before. He'd had some scrapes – Trigger the horse being only one example – and I'd seen a lot of pain on his face, but this was different; it was almost, you could say, haunted. I couldn't be sure, though, because there was a large swathe of bandage around his head and face.

"Tell you what, Saul, let's take it from the start. You were out on Great Western Road, right? Just out for a stroll, or going somewhere particular?"

"I was going down to The Comedians; I'd heard there was a meeting to discuss the Celtic supporters' bus which leaves from there, and what was to happen in the present crisis. It was a lovely day, so I walked. So, I'm on the left, going down, and I get well past Byres Road when I clock someone on the other side, about twenty yards ahead. I'm wearing my green jacket and he's wearing a green jacket; I mean the *same make* of jacket. I have brown cords on... and so does he. So far, so what? I speed up a little, to get to see the front view of this guy, but just as I'm pulling level, he stops at that second-hand bookshop, pauses and goes in. But not before I get a clear view of his face."

Saul stopped here and asked for some water. He was breathing quite heavily. Should I call for a nurse? In fact, I didn't need to, because one appeared, checked Saul briefly and said that maybe that was enough for him, for the time being. A doctor came by and also checked.

Saul croaked out to me: "Come and get me on Friday. Come and pick me up, right."

The doctor told me that the police had been involved, and of course had questioned Saul and the driver of the white van. They were satisfied that there was no criminal act committed, and the doctor knew of no charges being brought; Saul had suddenly just charged off the pavement at some speed, and hit the van almost immediately. His injuries were multiple but not serious, and he confirmed that they'd be letting him out on Friday morning, all being the same, at around eleven. It was now Tuesday.

But, when I turned up at Gartnavel on the Friday, I was told that Saul was already discharged, and someone had picked him up at about nine-thirty; they didn't know who. It was the same infuriating Saul of so many past scrapes: his own man, in his own way, marching to the beat of his own drum; folly and fun in equal measure. I knew he would be in touch, but I filed the memory of that powerful anxiety he'd displayed, when I visited him on the ward.

I did not have to wait long: the following night I was at the bar in The Palace, and had reached page 12 of *The Times*, when a hand clasped my shoulder and a voice whispered in my ear:

"Sorry about yesterday, John; it was necessary. Let's grab a table; there are too many people around this bar on a Saturday night."

We sat and I waited. Saul started to talk about somebody in the hospital – a visitor, maybe; not staff – who had been in to talk to him, but he just could not remember his name or who he was.

Dark Cloud then sauntered over and took Saul aside for a few minutes of conversation. When Saul returned, he looked a little less tense, even though that is rarely the effect of a conversation with Dark Cloud Phil. He waved back to Marta behind the bar and drew a deep breath.

"Right, so I was going down toward The Comedians… I don't drink during the afternoons now, but this looked a serious meeting, so I wasn't gonna miss it. Anyway, I notice this guy wearing my green jacket and brown corduroys, so I'm intrigued; he's across the road, also heading east. As I draw level with him, just before he goes into that bookshop, I see his face: it's a dead ringer for me! It *is* me! That's when, in utter shock, I step off the pavement and *BAM!* I'm unconscious.

"I saw *myself!* I was turning to go into a bookshop; it was definitely me, pale-blue shirt and all. This clear fact overtook everything else in my head, and I went to head across and get closer to this double. I didn't see any van; I didn't see any street; I just saw me!"

I tried to take in what he was saying, as he waited patiently for my response. For a minute, I didn't know where I was, and I double-checked: yes, this was The Palace of Mirrors. Along the wall, below the gilded name above the gantry, was etched in smaller letters: *"Come in and find out what you really look like."* Book-ending this invitation were two sculpted figures of soldiers with dog heads, maybe jackals. I wanted to just keep looking at this old, comforting scene; I wanted things to be the way they had been.

My daze did not last. If it happened just as Saul had described, then of course he might be shocked enough to step in front of a van. But then, maybe the idea of a "double" only came into his head after the accident. I was tempted to respond in a light tone at first, maybe along the lines of mock horror that there could be two identical Sauls going around Glasgow. Or, I could have played safe and gone for the old, "Were you wearing your glasses?" routine. But something warned me that this was not what was wanted; I realized that, if I was to get any more details out of Saul, I would need to be serious, rather than flippant. So, I placed my glass down slowly and, putting my hands to the sides of my face, I whispered:

"This is not just serious; this is terrifying."

"Terrifying, okay," whispered Saul, and went for a refill.

I did not know what my next move should be, but Saul had still more to reveal:

"That was twelve days before yesterday. So, I'm looking at me going into a shop in Great Western Road, then I'm being whisked away, patched up and mended – physically, anyway. But, during that healing period, how d'you think my brain was doing? What speed do you think it was at?

"Every day there were questions from different people; questions, questions, questions. Even my cousin Tom had questions when he came in; he looked a bit sceptical at my answers. I made sure that not once did I mention this double; I realized that was a dangerous move. Nobody there – not one of them – was going to believe that version. I did try it early on, with the doc, and he sent me for a brain scan; nothing came of that. For more than a week I lay there, tormented when I should have felt relieved, and should have been thankful. I was terrified!

"As the days wore on," (I had learnt from the hospital that he'd been there for over two weeks), "a particular idea kept coming to me; you could almost call it a plan—"

But, at this moment the monologue was broken, as Saul's pal Benny came in, gave Saul a wave and went to the bar. That meant Saul would be joining him soon, because they were close drinking buddies, and I would get back to reading the paper. Still, Saul was in no hurry, and he resumed the story.

"You've heard of a D.G., I suppose?"

"You mean a D.J.? Which one; there's a helluva lot?"

"No, no, a D.G.: a doppelganger. It's a foreign word; you must know it. It means an identical double, in German. It can happen to anybody. I don't know if we all have one, but many of us do. Right at this minute I know I have one."

"Right, so what's the purpose of this D.G.? I mean, why would there be two of just some people? How do they get here? Where do they come from?"

"Listen, my eyes have often deceived me, as the saying goes. I've seen a bus coming toward me, only to find out when it gets close that it's a truck. I've been in a shop queue and seen my aunt up ahead, gone over and tapped her on the shoulder, and said, 'Hello, Auntie Jane,' only to find that it is somebody else – somebody completely different. So, I know how eyesight can't be trusted. But I saw myself!"

"You said you had a plan, or were working on a plan? What's that?"

He glanced at me to check for sarcasm, but I gave him not a twitch.

"The last thing I remember is seeing the back of the D.G., as he went into the shop. Though, I couldn't swear that he actually did; he may have turned around, but it's probable that he went inside. Right? I myself have never been in that shop – never. The book-tender who works there, or whatever he is called, I have never seen, and he has never seen me – not in any recognizing way, I mean. So, if I was to go in there, I would expect to be totally unrecognized. If, on the other hand, the bookman said something like, 'Oh, hello again,' or, 'Did you like that last book you bought?' – well, it doesn't matter what he says; if he recognizes me, it's because on 23rd March he saw my D.G.

"Well, to be honest, I couldn't wait to try this out. So, yesterday morning, instead of waiting for you, I got a taxi and asked him to take me to the bookshop; I couldn't wait to get in there and find out the truth. But, when I got there, I got cold feet; I hesitated and asked the taxi driver to take me back up to Anniesland. But I can't shake it off. All I need is a little moral support."

"Ah," I said; I should have seen that one coming. "So, you want me to go with you, and we can find out if your so-called D.G. was really there – and maybe if he's a regular customer? That could be interesting."

"Yes, we go in, and from that moment I'm watching the book-tender like a hawk; I'll see any recognition.

"But, listen, give me a couple of minutes; just want to say hello to Benny."

"Sure. You gonna tell him… about the D.G.?"

"No way – well, not right now. I want to see where this goes before I start blabbing about it, and being the laughing stock of The Palace. No, only you know, and that's how I want it for now."

He slipped over beside Benny and Maggie, who claimed to be the oldest woman in Glasgow. She was in fact sixty-two, but maybe she felt like she'd been around a lot longer. She had been running a kind of campaign to have music in The Palace, but had always run into a brick wall. Her protests once got her barred for three months, which was a terrible disruption to the even tenor of her day, so she kept her protests rather mute nowadays.

I wondered: if we went into the shop and the book vendor did not even look at us, then we approached him and still he showed no recognition of Saul, then what? Would Saul accept that as proof? I didn't think so. Would he then query the chap or lady, asking if he or she had been on duty last Friday, and if not when Friday's attendant could be found back in the shop? Saul would surely then want to return for his date with destiny. If the book seller said, "Ah, hello again. How are you?" that would certainly be enough, and sure as doughballs Saul would be back, probing and seeking more info about the D.G., while plotting how not to give anything away.

After ten or fifteen minutes, Saul came back. I put down *The Times* and waited.

"S'okay. What I did there was explain about my bad hip, and how it just gave way suddenly that afternoon, and I couldn't help myself crumpling onto the road, meeting the white van side-on. Maggie wondered then why they didn't keep me in a lot longer, or transfer me to some orthopaedic place for surgery. So, I gabbled away about hospital priorities and pressures, and all that. Anyway, they're saying they want to go round and see Robin – you know, Robin McGregor. He's taken no' well; quite bad, in fact. Lungs, ah think."

"Round where? Where does he live?"

"No, not to his house; just through the back there, tae The Illusions."

"He's in here? He's round the back? But he's dying?"

"Good place to pass away, I'm sure you would agree. In fact, I think it might be something of a wee final session for Robin. There's a few round there with him already; maybe it'd be nice for us to raise a parting glass with him. Sociable, like; an old pal passing."

"God," I said, "it's as bad as that, is it?"

"Ye'll know when you see him."

All this talk about palaces and mirrors and illusions reminds me that I should hardly proceed further, until I provide some details about this tavern…

4

In the mid-1950s, the location was more of a restaurant than a pub, the bar being on a lower level. It was called The Station Bar (for the same bland reason as thousands of other Station Bars across the country). A settler from Chicago, named Samuel James Bowen, bought the premises and waded right in with a wrecking ball, ending the restaurant and making the bar, long and broad, the centrepiece of his new building. Then, he decided he needed a better name – little argument there – and (remember, this was 1956) decided he would personalize it from his own name. So, up in garish lights went the name *"SAMBO'S"*. That name lasted a couple of years (longer than it might have done nowadays). Bowen was not a redneck, but nor was he finely tuned to the rising calls for racial equality; still, he was a businessman, so he gave in. He took a further study of his name, and came up with an alternative which he thought would keep his ego afloat: down came *"SAMBO'S"* and up went *"JAMBO'S"*.

Now, Bowen, a Yankee with no interest in soccer, did not know that "The Jambos" is the nickname for Heart of Midlothian Football Club, but Hearts do not play in Glasgow; they are based in Edinburgh. And, Glasgow Celtic supporters, far from ostracizing this pub, seemingly renamed in honour of one of their greatest rivals, flocked in their multitudes, as a way of tormenting

Hearts fans further. Poor Bowen never stood a chance. "Flaming flamingos!" he cried, when the gaffe was explained. "I'm outa here! This city is even crazier than Chicaggy!"

Still, it was five years before he sold the place and disappeared. The new owner, Kathy Kelly, saw the funny side of it all and, to the surprise of many, insisted that the pub remain as "Jambo's". And that it did, for about twenty years. Celtic fans were happy to use it as a sort of western outpost in the city.

It was in the mid-nineties when Kathy, no longer fit to parade as the Calamity Jane of the West End, began to succumb to pressure from more than one of the big brewer corporations, and finally Waterfall's took over. Within a month, due notice given to all patrons and staff, they had closed the place down, with plans, they said, for significant refurbishment, which would "reflect both the history and the future of this grand establishment."

The results, predictably, divided opinion. Personally, I've always found the gold and silver exterior quite stunning, especially when it's facing a nice sunset, but "The Palace of Mirrors" seemed, to many, too pretentious a name for a Glasgow bar. Still, so it was named.

When ascending a flight of eight steps and stepping through the doors in front of you, through an archway on which was written, *"The Angels' Voices Whisper"*, you would come to a roomy, almost square lounge bar, with the inscrolled title: *"The Palace of Illusions"*. To your right, up a few steps, was a similar bar with longer tables, and again you would enter through an archway, upon which was embossed the words: *"The Souls of Previous Times"*.

To the left stretched the main bar, a long and spacious room, upon whose entry arch was inscribed not only, *"The Palace of Mirrors"*, but also, in smaller print below that: *"Come in and find out who you are"*. At each end of the bar itself was ensconced a carving of a soldier, with the head of a jackal-like dog. It was a long way from Sambo's, and even Jambo's.

Some patrons, mainly old geezers, bemoaned the strange and puzzling changes. Visitors, and some of the more inquisitive regulars, would seek information about the inscriptions and the overall theme, but none was forthcoming. A barman named Danny once told me that this was policy; staff were to provide no clues as to the significance of the artwork – as a rule, when faced with nosey questions, bar staff should simply say: "Enjoy your drink."

Anyway…

With Robin, it was certainly hard to tell if he was dying; he looked the same to me as he'd always looked. I'd been in his company only a few times, and thought him quite droll and perceptive, in the little he had to say. Two tables had been pushed together, and the group made way for Saul and me to squeeze in. Not my cup of tea; not one little bit.

"Hello, Saul," said Robin. "Ah heard ye knocked a van over. Wis it damaged?"

"Well, it was in a worse condition than you, you auld rascal! Performing the dying swan act once again, you rogue?"

This light, bantering note having been struck, the night relaxed around the company and we nattered away. Karl, a saturnine, scholarly fella, asked Saul when he'd got out of hospital.

At that, for some reason, Saul got a bit snooty. "I am not saying this again; I was released on Friday last. Please, let's leave it at that." So, we did.

The conversation pinballed about and the night drew on, Robin deteriorating only slightly. At one point, he said: "I would like to thank all nine of you for giving me a lovely night, which I hope to remember for many years to come." There were eight of us in the party, not nine; he mustn't have been counting himself.

Paying a toilet visit, I bumped into Karl. He asked if Saul was correct about his date of release from hospital.

"Definitely," I was able to assure him. "Why do you ask?"

"Naw, it's alright. It's just that, about ten days ago I was down that way, quite near Kelvin Bridge, and I saw a guy who looked very much like Saul; quite a resemblance, really. Though, of course, it wasn't Saul if he was in hospital."

"Right. As you say, there are lots of resemblances like that; you see them all the time: guys walking around the spitting image of Oliver Hardy or Rab C. Nesbitt."

Back at the party (or the wake, maybe), Maggie had started to sing. Feeling she was on safe ground, in the circumstances of Robin's farewell, she was halfway through *"Will Ye Go, Lassie, Go?"* – a dirge which was popular during the folk boom of the seventies. But, she had a sweet voice (oldest woman in Glasgow, remember), and she was joined in the refrains by a pleasant harmony from young Angela, Robin's granddaughter. All was merry and mellow; even Saul was twitching less than usual.

Lemmy also offered to sing, and since his songs usually lasted around ten minutes, Saul took the opportunity to communicate sotto voce:

"I was thinking about the different ways this might all pan out; maybe you've been giving it some thought, too? I bet you didn't see this as our gateway to fame and celebrity: me and my D.G. And you could be our... you know, manager, adviser; maybe even our P.R. guru."

This was surely a case of the drink talking. The mood of urgency in him had slipped. "Half an hour ago you were saying this was a world-class secret; now you want to take it onstage! Don't you have to do some serious investigating first?"

"I do, yes. When are you available? I was hoping Monday or Tuesday I might go into action."

"I'll have to check if my Action Man suit is back from the cleaners."

5

"Morning, gentlemen. How are we today? Rain's stopped, I see."

"We're fine, thanks. Taking a look, if that's okay?"

"Of course. Just ask if you need any help."

If ever a conversation can be said to write itself, it's the one between a bookstore assistant and his first customers.

At this point, Saul and I turned in toward each other by mistake. "Oops," I said, then saw what utter amateurs we were.

As luck would have it, Saul came across a work on playing the bagpipes, with the deadly title *Chanters of the Glens*, overpriced at two pounds. I nodded in encouragement and he went over to the counter.

"Is this the only book you have on bagpipe playing?"

"I believe so. To be honest, it's not one I know much about – hence the rather silly price."

Only then did Saul look him straight in the eyes, up close, but the friendly smile on the assistant's face did not flicker for an instant. Saul's plan was maybe not strongly enough worked out. We wished the man a good day and left.

"Well," I asked, "did he know you?"

"It's hard to say; I mean, he might have. Even if he recognized me, doesn't mean he's going to get excited every time I come in. On the other hand, I can't say that I saw anything more than general politeness." Saul was downcast. But he was a quick healer, and he was starting to throw off the effects of his injuries.

That was when I brought up the subject of his meetings, which had obviously been seriously neglected.

"That is now a problem," he admitted. "I was surprised at the number of people contacting me over the past coupla weeks, asking if I was okay, and why I hadn't been at the latest meeting. Shettleston Bowling Club were particularly disappointed, because apparently they had a wee special award for me; a surprise, you know. But what could I do?"

"You don't bowl. What sort of award would a bowling club be conferring on you?"

"Well, John, it turns out that you don't know everything. I can't travel, John, and for a while there I had different guys ferrying me around. But there's a limit to that; some of them didn't like sitting in a car for a couple of hours, while I followed the case for extending the allotments down at Scotstoun. Also, with this hip getting worse, and no remedy in sight for a long time, travelling to meetings is just getting too difficult. I do not like the prospect of spending all my time in The Palace, delightful as it is; I need to find something else, something new, to throw myself into."

Or under, I thought. Then I had another thought – or rather, a picture – of Saul sitting at a table in The Palace, maybe back in The Illusions, where it's a little quieter, and working from there to keep in touch with his meetings: writing letters, making phone calls, sending his views and suggestions in advance of the next meetings. He would miss the sparring of debate and the clash of opinions, so central to many meetings, but it might be a happy alternative. "Our great friend Saul cannot be here in person tonight, but he has written a letter to us, which I shall read out now," the secretary of the Springburn Wheeltappers' Association would announce. I chuckled and Saul raised his eyebrows, but now was not the time to reveal my brainwave.

"What now, o crazy one?"

"Well, that was inconclusive. I think now the chances are lower, but really nothing much has changed: the D.G. is around; only a couple of weeks have passed."

I had to interrupt: "Saul, it's four weeks."

He was unfazed; "Not the point. He's around here, and he will be back around here."

"You could put a camera up in one of those trees over there, and check it regularly. Obviously you cannot camp out here."

"Not for the first time, John, I am wondering if you are the right man for this; you can't help taking the mickey."

"I'm not! C.C.T.V. is all over the place nowadays. What's your plan?"

"John, a plan is something rational; something scientific. But, if this D.G. is real, then we are outside of scientific reality; we're into a mysterious other world, a new dimension. For all I know, this particular D.G. might come and go through a wormhole! You heard of them? Probably not. If the D.G. is real, and strolls along here one day, do you think he's going to pause and smile and wave for the camera? I would even wager that a D.G. would not appear on a camera."

We were still standing outside the bookshop, arguing like this, and I felt tired in my bones. Saul could have that effect; he could suddenly make you feel exhausted. His energy for ideas was amazing, but if you tried to keep up with it, you could come down in a heap.

"Saul, I have to go; I have some things to do. Next time I see you in The Palace, I bet you'll have it all sorted out. I'll only say take it easy; this could get on top of you. It could really change you."

When I left him, he was watching me with a funny look in his eye, and stroking his chin, maybe like Aristotle.

6

I had been away visiting my daughter for a bit, then began to suffer from a back problem, which would not respond to any therapy. I cut back on my trips to The Palace, but when I did visit I checked on Saul, from the usual barflies; they had no news of him.

Time passed and, with a little more breathing space, my writing was making some progress.

Then, one Thursday in May, out of the blue, Saul was standing beside me at a bus stop. He gave me quite a hug, and we picked up almost from where we had left off. But, only *almost*. He was different.

On the bus, going into the city centre, he sat in the seat behind me, and told me quite calmly and fluently about an aunt of his, who had just been locked up in a mental institution. Apparently, she had been a habitual shoplifter, but when she was finally caught had protested her innocence. She kept up this protest, even in the face of store camera evidence, and all the way through her court appearance; she insisted it was not her but somebody else who had been doing the shoplifting. She sought help from doctors and priests, but not from her husband (Saul's uncle) Bertie, who testified that she was always coming in with stuff in her bag that neither of them wanted or ate; it all got thrown out, mostly. "After all, who wants stuffed mushrooms or a bag of whelks?" Bert asked. Aunt Jane was committed to the care of some institution, out near Stirling.

Saul had just been to visit her, the previous day, and he told me this story in vivid detail, during the short bus ride. Saul was subdued and sympathetic in his narration – somewhat different in tone than he had been, when we last stood together and argued about the doppelganger. To conclude the story, he did add that the whole question of insanity was quite a mystery, since there was no history of such behaviour in Saul's family.

We got near to the city centre, so naturally I asked if he was off to a meeting. He chuckled a little and shook his head.

"Not in the way you mean. I am meeting somebody: a priest, who's having problems with the church organ; a mutual friend told him I had some knowledge of how pipes worked. So, before he goes ahead with very expensive repairs, he asked could I take a look at them. Not the same as bagpipes, of course, but I might identify some fault. Anyway, that's where I'm off to: down to Clyde Street, to the cathedral. What about you?"

"Also on a musical quest: I want to get a metronome. I'm learning the piano – or trying – and I believe the metronome is a good idea for keeping in rhythm. There are one or two shops I can try. After that, I'm heading up to the GOMA library. Look, there's the National Piping Centre."

The somewhat shabby building stood on Cowcadden's Street, and I recalled that Saul had once worked there.

"I know it well," he confirmed; "spent a lot of time there in my prime, you might say."

"When did you retire?"

"I *got* retired – well, thrown out, to be precise. I went on the rampage one Friday and burnt my bridges – just about burned down the centre, as well. I was younger then."

I tried to visualize Saul being manhandled down the flight of stone stairs we were now just passing – it was not too difficult. He didn't offer any further detail.

"Don't know how long I'll be. But I get the bus back from the stop just round from GOMA, so I'll look in; if you're still there we can have some tea."

As I strolled around in pursuit of a metronome, I remained rather stunned. Church organ? Tea? That didn't sound right. Crazy aunt, yes; that was much more in character. Going on a rampage? Certainly; that was in keeping with his personal history. But, tea?

I got a cheap metronome, and was just examining it, sitting in the GOMA tearoom, when in walks Saul with a priest.

"John, this is Father Dorman."

"David Dorman," said the priest, offering a handshake. "Tea for you, Saul?" The question was half-spoken, half-chanted, like some monk singing his plainchant.

"Nothing better," answered the maverick. Suddenly, the whole world was drinking tea.

We sat and sipped and parlayed for a while, about this and that, until Saul mentioned his Aunt Jane, who wanted to meet with Father Dorman. Jane claimed that she knew Dorman from a distant past, was able to name the parish where he had then been a curate, and said that he was one of the few people she could trust. She had told Saul that if anyone could help her it would be David Dorman.

David himself did not look too convinced. For one thing, he admitted he had no real memory of the lady, having encountered very many women over his years as a priest, though she might well simply have just slipped his memory. But, Jane had mentioned not only the parish – St. Theresa's – but the name of another priest who had been there at that time, which Dorman recognized.

Before we got any further into the story, David Dorman then stood up and said he had to go and check some results. He would give Saul a call the next day, to see what could be arranged for Aunt Jane.

"He's not a bad guy," said Saul, "but he's hard to read. I don't know; I can't make him out. He's going somewhere to check some 'results'? What results?"

"Football? Horses? An x-ray, maybe?"

"That's just what I mean: you're never quite sure where you are with him. Anyway, Jane certainly needs help, and she asked me to find Dorman, so I'd better leave it at that for now; see what comes of some priestly intercession. But, take my advice: watch out for that Dorman."

As ever with Saul, I was left to wonder why I should need to watch out; what was Dorman to me? Saul's attitude toward the priest was confusing. I had never known him rely on the uses of any priest, and we had attended the same Catholic school.

"What about the organ pipes? Did you get that sorted for him?"

"Nah. Don't even know why I mentioned that. It was a red herring, as they call it; nothing to do with organs. Sorry about that deception, old chum. There are some lies, you know, that are so stupid you just feel right ashamed. I just wanted to get help for Auntie; she was so kind to me. Anyway, maybe she is better off in that asylum than living with Bertie; he's the crazy one, not her. *He* should be locked up."

I wanted to press him more on the out and out deception of the organ pipes. Why would he think it necessary to lie about that? But then, his remark about Bertie being locked up threw me into a different thought.

"Did you ever go to any prison meetings? I mean, with prisoners, or about prisoners?"

"Musta done, sometime or other. I vaguely recall, over at Bishopbriggs, they tried a 'befriend a prisoner' scheme. Disaster; some volunteers got quite injured! No, if you're in prison, you're in prison 'til you're out – best get used to it."

This sounded a bit dogmatic. I tried another door to the topic: "You still getting to all those meetings?"

There was a pause.

"They're gone. Finished. Don't do any meetings now. Haven't got time, really. Aunt Jane, for example, is almost a full-time job, and she's not the only one; there's another aunt: Cora, Jane's sister… of course. Lives somewhere in Ireland, where long may she stay."

I waited, hoping to hear an explanation for this huge change of lifestyle, but none came. He'd had big problems with travel and mobility, but he'd always got around them. As always in earlier times, I somehow felt an urge to help Saul, to be useful to him. He was always wrestling with some difficulty or other, never at peace – though, who is?

"Well, anything I can do… Do you visit Jane often?"

"No, not much; I find her hard to understand. I want to be on her side, but she speaks in more than one language, if I can put it that way. She makes me kind of nervous."

"Did she do any shoplifting?"

"Well, all along she has stuck to her version of events, that somebody beside her put items in her shopping bag. When she was asked about earlier times she'd been caught, she now said it had always been the phantom shopper, but she hadn't liked to mention it. And, who on Earth would believe her? Her husband certainly didn't. On each earlier occasion, the items she got caught with were so cheap: like a carton of salt, and another time a clump of broccoli. Although, once she came home with a marzipan cake, which Bertie soon scoffed entirely. What she stole was a puzzle to everyone, and she would have probably got off lightly, even as a habitual offender, if she had simply owned up to it. But she stuck all the way, to the story of the shadow beside her which did the stealing, so that needed to be examined. And they're still examining her – only now she's in a cage."

"What?!"

"In a manner of speaking, I mean. She can't go home. Though, I must say, when I visit her she shows little enthusiasm for going home, anyway. Funny we're still talking about her.

Funny I met you today. Maybe you and Jane should meet." For the first time since we'd met up that day, Saul smiled. It seemed almost like a challenge.

"Well," I said, "a strange lady with a shadow following her? How can I refuse?"

7

The psychiatrist, or maybe she was the security guard, kept well back out of the way, so that I got a good, clear sight of Jane. Her skin was fresh and unlined, and her hair was shiny. She wore a full-length, green dress of some light material, possibly silk. She had a sort of Madonna-like presence, and reminded me a little of a saintly aunt of my own: Aunt Annie, now long gone, but strikingly similar in my memory to the woman who stood before me now.

I had rehearsed a few openings, as you do, but they seemed pathetic. So, I told her straight off: "You remind me of my Aunt Annie. She's dead now, but she was lovely, especially in a spiritual way."

"Are you trying to pay me a compliment? What do you mean? Did she ever steal anything, or did someone else do the stealing?"

"I think she stole some pears once," I bizarrely found myself saying.

Jane clapped her hands; "Bravo! Pears! That's a good start. Oh, I think I am going to enjoy this. Now, sit down and let's get to know one another. How long have we got? Do you know?"

"Well, I think about forty minutes. Saul agreed to let me come in first, while he… does something else, then he'll have forty-five minutes with you."

"Yes, yes, but I see him all the time; you're a special treat! He can have his forty minutes next time. I wanted him to bring the priest and now he has, and here you are. You're younger than I expected. Pleased to meet you, Father Dogman."

It was one of those frozen moments you read about. I was seriously tempted, though only briefly, to reply: "How do you do, Jane?" Fortunately, I did no such thing. And Dorman looked nothing like me.

"Sorry, Jane, but I think you've made a mistake. I think you mean Father Dorman."

"Dorman, yes, of course. Easy mistake to make."

"But I'm not him. I'm not Father anybody; I'm not a priest. I'm John, a friend of Saul's for many years. I don't suppose he's ever mentioned me."

"I'm getting very confused. How on Earth can you help? What are you doing here, anyway? Where is Saul?"

"Saul's in the café, I think. Father Dorman couldn't manage today, so Saul asked would I like to come over for the run. He does this quite often; gives him support, maybe."

"So, I need Saul's support, and Saul needs your support, and no doubt there'll be someone supporting you… and so the world goes round and round. You look like a priest – well, a bit like a priest. D'you want to pretend?"

"Okay, let's pretend. What are we going to pretend, exactly?"

"Well, you will have to hear my confession, of course. I've got a lot of sins to pay for… Maybe this is not quite the moment for confession; let's slow it down a bit. D'you have any strong drink on you?"

"No, sorry. If I'd known—"

"Known what? That I was a dipso? Ha-ha, never mind! I have my own sources. Ha-ha! Oh dear, you're looking quite frightened – or is that just puzzled? I'm so glad Saul comes to visit me, but he gets puzzled so easily and I can't resist. Am I being naughty? Should I confess that sin? Ha-ha-ha! Oh, dear. Just think what we'd be like if you had brought some hooch. I had a fancy recently for Navy rum – you know, the dark stuff the sailors drink? That, with a wee skoosh of blackcurrant, and the party can get started."

She was an absolute hoot, this lady, and seemed to be growing even hootier. I was beginning to enjoy her company and relax. I had come with some questions for her, but I realized now how useless they would be. She was way beyond smarter than me, anyway, and drank from a well of untainted lunacy.

"Let's sit down. I can't see too well, and that's usually a bad sign. My eyesight has a secondary function, which is to warn me of more distant dangers; it seems to be warning me just now. Perhaps you are dangerous? Would you say you were a dangerous person, Mr. John?"

"Certainly not to you, my dear; you have nothing to fear from me."

Then she shifted the whole tone, and began to ask me simple, normal questions, which people of slight acquaintance do: where was I born; what did I work at; did I have a family? All that stuff. I fell in with that and put some easy questions to her, about her younger days, and her favourite films and books. Nothing sensational was revealed, but one interesting point she mentioned was that her husband Bert had been married before, and his first wife had died. He disliked talking about that time, Jane said. Once, she came across a photo of the dead wife, Valeria, and got quite a fright when she saw how close the resemblance was between them. I found this interesting, as well as another remark she let slip out, when at one point she said, with a smile which was quite sly:

"You know, John, these people, they'll believe anything. You know, I could tell them whatever I liked, whatever came into my head, and they'd believe it."

She could have been wrong, of course, or deluded, but I wanted her to tell me more about this. Unfortunately, our time was up, and at that moment the security guard rang a tiny bell, with a very sweet chime, perfectly pitched, to announce the ending of a visit.

At the door, Jane clasped my hands in hers. They were ultra-soft, like a seal. "I hope you'll come and visit me again."

"Yes. But maybe you won't be here."

"A-ha, so you have been talking to those quacks behind my back?!" She was smiling when she said this.

"Of course not. As if they would tell me anything about a patient, anyway."

"You haven't really been listening, John. Never mind. I'd better get my eyeshadow touched up for Saul; he likes a bit of glamour, as I'm sure you know."

In the ten-minute break between visitors, I was able to chat with Saul, who seemed nervous and anxious.

"What was she like, John?"

I didn't really know the answer to that question. For forty minutes this enigmatic woman had waltzed rings around me, bamboozled me, and kept it all seeming as normal as afternoon tea at the vicarage in late May.

"She was funny, Saul; she was funny. I don't know why on Earth she is in this place."

"Is she unhappy?"

"She's funny," I repeated; "funny and unhappy don't usually go together."

"Did you mention me?"

"A little, but nothing serious."

"Was she funny about me?"

"No. She said you liked glamour."

"Glamour? What on Earth were you two talking about? Glamour? Heavens! She's my aunt!"

"Exactly, and she's glad you've come to see her. So, make her happy."

The building was set in pleasant parkland, and I took a little stroll while Saul was visiting Jane. There were vivid shrubbery and walkways under arching trees, with a little plate which read *"The Laburnum Archway"*, and a pond set in a lovely lawn; it was designed with skill, and very soothing. I sat on a bench and tried to work out the Jane story, but kept running into walls. On one reading, she was surely not in the right place, but simultaneously her elusive and profound behaviour might well suggest dangerous undercurrents. Maybe I was looking too closely, and Saul would have more skill at getting to the heart of the matter.

I was still sitting on the bench, deep in thought, and not noticing the time passing, when I decided that there had to be some quite high security here. It was well hidden, though; no barbed wire, no walls with turrets, and certainly none of those *"NO WARNING SHOTS"* signs American correctional centres are fond of.

When Saul found me, it was clear that he had been crying and was trying to regain some composure. He sat down at the far end of the bench, like I was contagious – or maybe like he had been spooked. I just waited.

"I had to remind her that my mother is dead; she died years ago," he told me. "She ignored that and said something like: 'The key is jammed in the lock, 'til Saul finds the son of Barbara.' Barbara is my mother's name, so it must mean something… like ''til I find myself.'

"I tried to make sense of Jane, but it was no use. I thought she'd be getting out of here soon, but now I'm not so sure. I saw signs of definite insanity, so you can bet that the doctors will, too. They'll not release her; she might be a danger to herself or others – especially Bert. She said she'll never return if he's there; said he was crazy. She asked me again to get Father Dorman to come and see her. That Dorman, though, there's something not right about him."

"She thought at first that I was Dorman."

"She's far gone. Let's go."

8

Three nights later, Saul made his comeback at The Palace. He was welcomed quite riotously by those who knew and liked his off-the-wall reputation, yet others stayed quiet and hardly acknowledged him. He didn't seem to care either way. He said he hadn't had any alcohol for two months, and was about to catch up.

Young Bernie giggled. She had a heart of gold and a head of lead, and so was extremely popular. Her own taste in men lay mostly in the over-forties, and that certainly included Saul. Bernie'd had a few by this time, and judged it fitting to throw her arms around Saul's neck and give him a kiss. He instinctively went to give her breasts a squeeze, then just in time thought better of it.

The company settled down a little, and wondered what they were now about to hear. Quite a few of us realized that fact and fiction were identical twins for Saul. He liked to say things like: "Facts are always false, and from fiction do not differ." He liked expressions which had a ring or a swing to them. He read a lot of poetry, and surprised us often with the phrases and lines he could quote. He was also fond of the lyrics of Sinatra and Gershwin, and liked to decorate the conversation with a snatch of song from the American Songbook. Then, just when we thought it was all a bit old-fashioned, Saul would remind everyone that the greatest ever composer in the history of popular music was Andrew Lloyd-Webber.

Everybody at the table had plenty to say, and I had time to look around and think of that night months earlier, when we said goodbye to Robin. The drink was getting me rather sentimental, and I said to Jack, who was presently no doubt hoping for an appointment with Bernie or her pal Sonya:

"Remember old Robin? He was a droll customer. Very good sense of humour for an old geezer. Were you in that night when we had a wee farewell session for Robin?"

Jack pointed to the far end of the room. There, in a snug corner, not too far from the bar, sat Robin with two chums. For once, the expression "like death warmed up" was apt; even from here I could see that Robin's face was the purest white, with coal nuggets for eyes. Maggie was beside him, and Wee Johnny Blanco. Johnny headed for an order at the bar, so I took a chance to join him and ask how things were.

"Hiya, John. Haveny seen ye in a while. Ah see Crazy Horse is back on the prairie. Whit's his latest wheeze? Thought we'd no' see him in here again, after that last rumpus."

I shook my head, having no idea what he was referring to. I had a question of my own for Wee Johnny: "How come Dracula's still among us?" I nodded toward Robin. "Three months ago we were lowering him into the earth, and now here he is, still. Could maybe do with a wee brandy, though; put some colour in them cheeks of his."

Wee Johnny laughed. Strange, but he always found me funny –

or, at least, he always thought whatever I said was meant to be a joke. "Heh-heh-heh, he's certainly wan o' they undead; the creatures that canny die. Used tae see them a lot in the cinema. They wanted tae die but they couldny."

"What's stoppin' Robin?" I asked. "He's no robin redbreast."

This flummoxed Wee Johnny Blanco and he laughed again, with some wheezing thrown in as a tip, and turned away to get his drinks ordered.

I took to musing about The Palace and its denizens; so many weird and wonderful characters in one bar. Drawn back to Robin, I went into a fantasy about reviving the vampire movie genre, here in Glasgow; Robin would be central, as long as he didn't have to stand up. Maggie and Wee Johnny Blanco were suitably nutty for parts as assistants to the Lord of Darkness; Bernie and Sonya would certainly help with the sensual and lurid aspects; and Saul might be some kind of ogre, though that might be slipping into some different genre.

I heard Sonya asking Bernie: "Did you put down 'curvy' in your *Match.com* profile? Or did ye go for 'chubby'?"

"Cheeky bitch! Anyway, 'chubby' wisnae wan o' the options; it mighta been 'cuddly'. 'Curvy' wiz certainly the nearest wan for me, though," was Bernie's stout reply. I rethought my casting fantasies.

At that moment, Saul's hand rested on my shoulder, and he whispered theatrically: "So… zhou arr watching ze wimmen… and zhou arr thinking, fitch wan first?"

"Hi there, old Saul. What age are you now? Passed the three-hundred mark yet? I had forgotten that vampire impersonation was one of your many skills. Pity you don't put some of the others to use," I added a little sourly, realizing I was getting drunk.

"Jane's preliminary health meeting is on Wednesday; it could be important to what they decide to do with her. D'you want to come? She liked you, I could tell. And Dorman's supposed to be there – if he turns up. I don't like that prick!

"Anyway, Sonya there was just telling me she had a twin. Would you believe that? Two Sonyas in one place would drive anybody bifocal."

The following afternoon I called Saul, because I had no memory of the details. I was advised that Dorman and Saul, and maybe Bertie, would pick me up at nine o'clock on Wednesday.

When Wednesday came, because Bertie was late, Saul phoned to ask me to make my own way to the hospital.

I caught up with them at the entrance, where the receptionist glanced at me across the top of her spectacles. *Very Hollywood,* I thought. She asked if I was kin.

"Sort of."

"Are you related to Mrs. Swift?"

"No."

"That's a problem, I'm afraid. Mr. Terry, did you not understand the regulations?"

I felt like asking how come the vicar had privileges that I didn't, but I knew it would be pointless. Bertie had been held up, and now Saul had phoned to apologize, saying I'd have to come on my own; he'd understand if I pulled out.

But I was fascinated by the lady, and this crime story, and I wanted to be in on the developments. So, I met the three musketeers in the reception area, and for a while we had some disjointed conversation. Bertie was a beanpole; who knew where he could have stashed all the food he was alleged to eat? I handed him a bar of chocolate, allowing him to snap off a piece; he ate the whole thing in two bites. Remarkable. From a very different world than Jane.

A girl with a clipboard approached us with a sunshine smile, and checked who we were. She ticked three boxes, then looked at me. "And you, sir? Are you of the party?"

"I am, but I don't meet the regulations. It's fine, go ahead. I'll wait around and catch up when you guys come out."

Clipboard Kate seemed relieved and flashed me a molar. As she led them away, I sat and took in the promenade, which was quite busy at this time of day. A few minutes later she reappeared and sat down, thanking me for being so reasonable. She then gave me a look which I could easily have misinterpreted, like she was sussing me out a little.

When her buzzer sounded, she stood for a moment and said: "Back in a minute."

I noticed her clipboard was left on the bench beside me, and I lifted it slightly to have a peek. That was when I reached what some refer to as a fork in the road.

Jane Swift's picture was there, beside her name, her date of birth and some other details. Then, below that:

"Next of kin: Robert (Bert) Swift."

If Miss Flirty had come back right then, a lot might now be different. But she did not.

As I looked down again at the sheet, I saw:

"Family:
"Nephew: Saul Terry, 1026 Crow Road, Glasgow, G13.
"Nephew: Peter Terry, Rockcliffe Holdings, Colvend, G56."

I put the clipboard back carefully and sat for a few minutes in amazement. At first, I was questioning myself: *So Saul has a brother? So what? He doesn't want the news spread around, and he's certainly been keeping it well concealed. We all know what he's like: full of surprises.* Then, I wondered: *What if Saul doesn't know he has a brother?*

Kate (name on badge) came back, just as I stood up. I asked her to tell my friends that something urgent had come up, and that I would get in touch later. Then I made my way out to the car.

9

I brooded for a bit. To that brooding I added a little shame, that I hadn't waited to see how things went for Jane. But my mind had gone elsewhere.

I knew something was going to be revealed, and my gut instinct was that it would be unsavoury. It's just that feeling you get; one of the few signs you can trust. I avoided The Palace, seeking my medicine in a bar a mile away, named (by some misinformed communist in the 1920s) The Two Shovels. The name was a beacon for those who wrote dirges about the Death of Capitalism, and thought it treasonous to drink anything other than draught beer.

After a few weeks, I realized that Saul was not looking for me, and I had somehow kept out of touch with him. Then it dawned on me that he was steering clear of me.

One evening, at about 9.30, I was in The Shovels, minding my business and watching some football, but feeling the time dragging. I looked around at the clientele: serious and gloomy, with the weight of the planet on their shoulders. I had a sharp pang of longing for the Palace of Mirrors.

When I arrived there, I got that old black magic feeling, walking up between the dog soldiers, a little guilty that I had been unfaithful, taking my feelings elsewhere. I almost expected one or two rebukes for my infidelity, but of course no one gave a hoot or said a thing. Martha behind the bar allowed her eyes to flicker in welcome, but that was as far as it got. No Saul, thankfully, but Karl had news.

"Hi. Where you been? Somebody said you wiz deid. You disappeared affa the horizon. Bam-boom."

From this, I estimated that Karl was probably on his fourth pint. So, I knew I could let him rattle away, and not have to ask too many questions.

"Ah don't think you know this, but no' only wiz ah at the Academy, like youse wiz, but ah wiz close behind; you and Crazy Horse were jest wan year in front a me."

"Actually, I do remember you. You were good at cards and card tricks, eh? You were always up for a game of cards. Yeah, I was closer to you than I was to Saul at school. Really, nobody was close to him. That could still be true."

"Aye, you and me got on awright, so we did; you're right. He's a wild card, I might huv said. I've tried to get closer to him ower the years, but it never came to much. He's pleasant enough tae me – though wan time he conned me intae buying somebody's doocot; ye know, a pigeon loft. Told me they were champion pigeons, and the guy's arthritis meant he had tae retire. Ah gave him two-hundred quid for that bloody loft and birds. Three months later they were a' gone. Saul laughed hysterically at that. He did gie me fifty back – 'compensation', he said – but ah wiz displeased. He pit moves like that on other punters, tae. Told an American tourist he had shares in the People's Palace doon oan Glesga

Green, and could sell some shares on tae the Yank for a hundred dollars. Tourist coughed up and Saul did a runner. Ah think his whole life's been like that: wasted."

Some of this I had heard before, but it had never mattered a lot. Whatever benefits Karl had got from being educated at the Academy did not seem to have transferred well into his later life. Same could be said for Saul, of course, and maybe that was Karl's point.

"He got upset wan night in here, no' that long ago, tellin' us aboot families an' things. Said he felt very bad aboot lettin' you down again – y'know, aw that drivin' and runnin' aboot you've done for him; felt very ashamed. But then kinda clammed up and widnae say whit wiz the cause o' this emotional upheaval. D'ye want tae know whit Saul lacks? Equilibrium."

"Did Saul say how his auntie is?"

"Naw... well, no' tae me. He disnae trust me much. But Maggie might know; she's roon' in The Illusions."

"How come?"

"She disgraced herself at the weekend; got in a fight, though ah think she wiz in the right. Some rat tried tae pinch her purse. There was a hullabaloo; there was blood, the outcome being that Maggie wiz nearly exonerated, but told to stay away from the front bar 'til further notice. So, she's roon' there. She might be on her own – though ah doubt it, knowin' Maggie."

"Hello, John, this is my Aunt Polly. Polly, this is John."

"Cheers, John, good luck to ya. Are you going to join us?"

Aunt Polly spoke in a pronounced Dublin accent, and had a twinkle in her eyes as she raised her wine glass toward me. She looked twenty years younger than Maggie, but then so did all women. I sat down opposite them.

Maggie seemed in a philosophical mood, so I raised a question. "Maggie, you know Saul; I heard somebody say that what Saul lacks is equilibrium. What's your opinion of this matter?"

"I do not have an opinion of this matter. He's off-balance most of the time, ah wid say, but since we're all much the same, there's just not enough evidence to start citing equilibrium as his central flaw. Most people say he's crazy, and that might be as far as we should go. Some people I've heard say he's worse than crazy; that he's into some bad stuff. Ah know you're a good help tae him."

"Is Saul a patron of The Palace?" asked Polly, and Maggie brought out the usual reply:

"He's an irregular regular."

"How quaint. Perhaps I will get to meet him and have a chat. I know a thing or two about equilibrium; I'm right well known for my expertise on the subject. It's a quality much in demand where I come from – and now. Will the bold Saul be joining us tonight?"

"Well, Polly, normally that would be easy for me to answer, but as is well known I am unjustly banished to this backwater, all because somebody tried to steal my purse; I am barred frae the main bar. And Saul never really comes down here, does he, John?"

"No. But I haven't seen Saul for a few weeks, so I don't know when he'll be back. If he was in The Mirrors, I'd tell him there's a lady waiting to meet him."

"Is that me or Polly you're referring to? You could say there are two ladies waiting to meet him."

"I've just had a good idea," added Polly: "we could be – Maggie and me, that is – his Yin and Yang. There's nothing better for an unbalanced person. We would not be wanting to cure him or anything – I'm sure he's much too interesting for that; we'd want to have some fun first. Then, maybe patch him up a bit, restore his equilibrium. I'm beginning to get excited about this.

"Listen, John, would you ever see me glass gets a refill of that lovely Merlot?" She raised her glass, now suddenly empty. I took it, and Maggie's, and headed back to the bar.

Barman Kevin informed me that Paddy Two-Sticks had been asking for me. Kevin smiled; he knew what that meant.

"How much this time?"

"Twenty."

Two-Sticks regularly ran out of cash, and when he did he would ask me for a loan. Always me, nobody else, and always by way of one of the bar staff. I knew I would get it back before the week was out, so I handed over a twenty to Kevin to pass on. It was no worry; Paddy had never failed to repay the loans.

Back to The Illusions with the wines, Maggie had gone to put on eyeshadow, and Polly gratefully accepted the large glass of Merlot I passed to her.

"You're a darling man, for sure," she breathed, in a rich and husky Dublin accent. I recognized that type of rich and husky, and kept my distance.

Polly expressed a great liking for the bar, and said it suited her very well. Though she had one improving suggestion to offer: there really should be some music – live, if possible.

Maggie returned, towing a younger lady she wanted Polly to meet. Quite sensual, even if her curves were no longer modest; quite a kind and relaxed face, too. Nice. She gave Polly a hug and a kiss, then looked at me.

I assured the ladies that, if Saul came in, I would ask him to come over. The young woman looked startled.

"Saul, did you say? I know Saul. Well, I bet there is only one Saul. You mean Saul's here? I knew Saul; we had a thing going – just a little fling, you know. Then we were kind of in business together, then he vanished. I'm Lydia, by the way; I'm in the purple-dye trade. Oh, Maggie, do you remember that time my heart got broken? That was Saul. He was an idealist, like Plato."

"Plato? Plato from Greece?"

"You know any other Platos?"

This gave me the chance to make a getaway, so I left with a little joke about three ladies around a cauldron. Maggie gave me a blank stare.

And there was Saul. It was 9.30.

He seemed quite bullish, as if his luck had turned. He also looked friendly, so maybe the time was right to try to re-install our bond. After all, I had walked out on him, at a moment he might well have benefitted from my support. Saul must have been of the same opinion, because he greeted me very warmly.

"John, you crazy Arab, it's good to see you. Listen, let me finish this business here with Phil, then you and I can have a wee talk… catch up. Plan ahead, maybe."

I went to my usual place at the bar and drank. A few minutes later, Phil, seemingly on his way out, put a hand on my arm and said:

"John, watch him; he's insane. Be careful."

Soon, the Black Knight himself was standing beside me. I'd had several plans of approach for this moment. For weeks, the subject of Saul's brother had been burning away at the back of my mind. I'd tried out a few openings, but none really convinced. So now, as usual, I just let the brook run where it would.

"First, John, Aunt Jane is still in that place; still in that asylum – cos that's what it is. The panel listened to Bert and me and Dorman, then informed us that their unanimous counsel at this time was for Jane to remain where she was."

"Saul, I'm not sure if that's a bad idea. When I saw her, and chatted and listened to her, I saw she was content, and even thought she was quite pleased with herself, for the way she had managed to get herself in there. She seemed quite at home – maybe a lot more at home than with that Bert; I didn't take to him one little bit."

Saul hinted to me about one or two projects he'd been tied up in. I paid little attention, having been here so often. The one about being neighbourhood vigilantes struck me as more of a risk than a fantasy. I thought it was time to revisit the doppelganger affair; that was surely unfinished business.

But then, from nearby, the noise of women singing in different keys brought us to a halt. Saul guessed that Maggie would be among them, and that made up my mind.

"Saul, have you ever been to a meeting in here?"

"Sure I have – long ago, though. As you know, I've cut right back on meetings; getting too much. Anyway, meetings here would have been too close to home. I'll explain that some other day."

"Let's have a little meeting just now. Come on, there are women waiting for you in The Illusions: three women. I'm not kidding. I did promise them that if you came in I would point you in their direction. That was them singing, I believe. Follow me."

10

Three quite different women, each looking at Saul in quite different ways. The Saul I knew would have taken the initiative and broken the ice with ease, but Saul looked stumped. His eyes moved between the ladies, as he sought an opening for a situation that was too much for him. He took a seat on the curved, padded bench and I moved in beside him. I was determined not to help him out this time.

Maggie stepped in: "Saul, this is Aunt Polly. She's from over the water. We've been telling her about you, so be on your best behaviour. And this is Lydia."

There was a dramatic kind of pause, while Lydia made up her mind whether she was indeed looking at the Saul she'd once tangled with in an earlier constellation.

But Saul had started to recover his poise – or maybe his nerve. "Lydia from the purple-dye trade? You wear it well. Good to see you."

Lydia chuckled, but kept her cards held high and close. "The purple-dye trade is not the mystery it once was; everybody's at it now."

"Not me, not me; I got enough on my plate. Just don't have the time for that trade anymore."

"Just as well, for it's not purple anymore."

Maggie, Polly and I were spectators at this little piece of theatre. We knew the words but not the meanings. From the way they dealt with one another, Polly and Lydia seemed to be acquaintances, yet Saul was brand new to Polly, so there were more hidden streams running merrily along. Maggie was an entire stream of her own, of course.

When Kevin appeared to announce to her that her ban was over, that her sentence was served and she could use the Mirrors bar as she wished, Maggie was hoopla-doopla. A few others came round to join in the celebration, and it had all the makings of yet another party at The Palace.

Usually, I would have been one of the first to leave these occasions, which could get far too boisterous. There were always recriminations, next day or next week; grudges and resentments were common – all the undercurrent of drinking culture, in which Glasgow leads the field. But I thought this time I would stay longer. Both Polly and Lydia were fascinating and maybe, if I watched and listened, I would learn. Because, I could not escape this sense that there was something I had to learn about Saul. It was important, yet always just out of reach.

At this point, I looked around and had a recurring idea that The Palace was beginning to change its character… or lose its character. Maybe Maggie had read my thoughts, because she articulated what I was musing over:

"You see that girl down there in the black hair, red dress? I happen to know her. She's only sixteen and she's drinking cider. The rest of those with her will all be about the same age. This place is getting much too lax, and too much of an under-twenty-five club; too scared to lose the custom of the youngsters, who don't care how much they spend. It's bad; the place could get shut down."

Polly nodded, vigorously. "How right you are. So, let's make hay while the sun is shining."

After a few drinks, you change everybody knows it. When Saul headed to the bar, I followed him. As soon as he had ordered, I gripped his wrist.

"Isn't it time you levelled with me? Remember the doppelganger? All that stuff you dragged me through, and now it's history? Or maybe you've forgotten the psycho condition you were in at that time; you walked into the road and got hit by a van. Have you just erased that whole experience?" I was trying to speak quietly, but the bar was crowded and I had to raise my voice. I could see one or two listening to this, maybe hoping for a barroom bust-up – unusual on a Wednesday night, even for Glasgow.

Saul realized that others were watching, and he seemed to tighten up, maybe even panic a little. Then, something happened; his eyes narrowed and he was licking his lips. When a thin guy beside him started to snigger, Saul pushed him in the chest, and snarled something at him I didn't catch. And, in true Keystone Cops tradition, that was how it started; the rammy spread instantly, and in minutes several people, including me and one innocent-looking woman, were on the floor – I realized it was Lydia on the sawdust beside me. It didn't last more than about two minutes, but there was some blood on shirts, a few broken lips and bruised ribs.

I escorted Lydia back round to Polly and Maggie, who were singing a low duet, in some other universe. Even when they saw us staggering toward them, they completed the song verse before stopping, asking why they had missed all the fun. Like most people in drink, they thought they were brilliantly funny.

"I was just wanting a few words quietly with Saul," Lydia explained.

You're not the only one, I said to myself.

"Somebody barged into me and elbowed me in the side. When I swung back, I knocked a drink over. Next thing I knew, I'm going down – you can't box in these shoes – but I'm okay."

Normality returned with surprising speed. I expected a few guys would be fingered and barred, maybe including Saul. But, no; ten minutes later he sauntered round to The Illusions – tried to play it off as a joke, but nobody was buying that. Polly started into a little Irish ditty, about Skibbereen or somewhere, and that relaxed everybody. Though Saul's attempts to hide his gloom were a poor effort.

An hour later we were all poleaxed, but maudlin and friendly – except once, when Maggie made a mess of trying to join in on one of Polly's republican ballads. After the song was over, Polly asserted that, had she not been in full voice, she would have given Maggie "such a whack". By this time, Polly's eyes were in a permanent squint, but she was still half-focused on Maggie when she advised: "You have to know your song well before you start singing!"

Half-drunk as I was, I could survey the wreckage with some insight. What was this place coming to? But it wasn't the place, it was the people who were in it: like myself; like Saul. I thought we seemed to have fallen extremely low. I could not think why, and could not think what could be done about it.

Funnily, my concern once again was with Saul, rather than with myself. Only a few hours earlier, Phil had warned me about Saul – the latest in a line of such warnings. Why did I so want Saul to be better than he was? More than once that evening, he and Lydia were very close and intense, as they discussed something private to them. It seemed clear that she was very drawn to him, and that he was not returning the feeling.

Through the fog came a scene from long past…

We were back at school, about sixteen and in the same class – friends, but not close. There were ten of us doing Higher Latin, and we were waiting for Dermott, our ancient teacher, to show up. Scholars that we were, we fell to insulting each other, which soon graduated into the usual slurs about mothers: "Your maw's a darky" was popular then; so was: "You're the spittin' image of oor postman." Mothers were easy targets, because mothers were prized and valued.

Even then, Saul had quite a solid personality, but never loud. So, when Saul quietly added to the jamboree…

"I don't have a maw; don't have a mammy. No family whatever, except for two aunties, no' much older than me. None of you can beat that, I'll bet."

…this revelation really was a shock.

In the times before Facebook, it was still quite easy for a schoolboy to keep secrets about his family. Saul didn't say: "My ma is dead"; it was simply as if he'd never had a mother. And two aunts, not an aunt and an uncle? What on Earth was this kind of set-up? Plus, for teenagers with ripe imaginations, what to make of the aunts being just a little older than Saul? This had us in a whirl.

But, before anyone could start probing, in tottered Dermott with his time-worn copy of *The Aeneid.* I felt a deep sympathy – almost like sorrow – for Saul; the feeling has never really gone away.

During this period, my marriage had finally gone belly-up and I was making a fresh start. My three daughters kept in close touch, but were getting a little vexed because, every time they called, I seemed to have something bad – or, at least weird – to report about Saul. My girls' advice varied: one said to cut him away, or I would never really restart; another said that if I still believed, then I should help him and stick with him; the third said I should get him psychiatric treatment. I tried to juggle the advice, and I was wearying, but the call of loyalty remained strong.

And, anyway, the dialectic was about to change.

PART TWO

11

I met this gal, Patricia. We became close friends. She came from Washington, long before, but had lived among us for years. Crow-black curls, and eyes as green as her grandmother's native land. We met on an online service known as *Match.com*, liked each other, and things started to settle down quite well. To keep my new start untainted, I did not burden Patricia with any of the history of me and Saul.

I could not help showing my affection for the Palace of Mirrors, though, but she was unimpressed; she said it was a dump, where tweedy women fell off of barstools and did a weird dying donkey death-dance on the floor – Patricia was real good at phrases like that.

Another time, we were again debating the merits of my favourite place, when she said: "D'you know Bob Dylan?"

"I've heard of him," I said; "an American. Why? What's Bob Dylan got to do with it?"

She found this extremely amusing. She said: "I'm not telling you. If I tell you, will you promise to stop going to that place?"

"No. Impossible; too much to ask. Sorry."

"Okay, fine. You'll find out, and you'll come crawling and grovelling. I'll make a deal with you: I'll tell you at the Changing of the Guard." I loved the way she would say cryptic things like that.

With a new interest in my life, I was now on a break from my erratic companion Saul. But it was not in the Great Plan that we should part early.

One sunny day in early July, I was taking a stroll with Patricia, down through the Botanic Gardens. The place had a nice buzz. People liked to sit on the lawns, so there were plenty of vacant benches. I saw a man with a familiar face, and kept looking at him as we sauntered along. As we drew aside his bench, he knew I'd been looking; he waved and said:

"It's you, John! Long time no see."

As before, the words were chanted, as if in keeping with the rules of plainsong – which was funny, since most of the time he was examining Patricia with greedy eyes. I did that silly finger-snapping thing, which is meant to signify jogging your memory, then it hit me:

"Dorman! Father Dorman."

"Not so loud, John."

I was astonished. He wore a green silk, open-neck shirt and white chinos, though at least he had Jesus sandals on. He also had a crew-cut. He looked ridiculous.

"Sorry. It's just that, last time I saw you, you were a bit less colourful."

He chuckled and waved us to sit down, which we did.

"So, are you on holiday? Or…" I was struggling.

"Isn't it a lovely day to be soaking up some sun? John, who is this charming companion you have?"

"This is Patricia. She's a friend of mine."

"Yes, I see. How are you, my dear? John and I had some business together, a while back… never got it finished, somehow. Awkward case."

Patricia smiled and waited.

I decided to call Dorman's bluff: "Sorry, Father, I do remember you, but to tell the truth the details escape me. Did we have a mutual friend in some distress, or something like that? My memory is befuddled."

Dorman wasn't falling for it. But, after a long pause, he gave a defeated sigh. "He's in bad shape; he has gone downhill. What friends he had have disappeared; he now seems to have one or two new friends, though they don't seem very people-friendly, so he's mostly on his own. I check in on him now and then, to see how he's doing."

Dorman's frankness affected me. Suddenly, again I wanted to know how Saul was, and how I might help. Patricia seemed to intuit this, and did not intervene when I said: "Is it possible to meet up with him? Anything you can arrange?"

"Give me your phone number," said Dorman, "then just wait. You might need to be patient, though; he's not well: his sight is poor. As I said, I go over to see him, but he's not interested in visitors – at least, he's not interested in me. And, he still has not paid me for any of last year's jobs."

I did not understand that. Perhaps Dorman was kind of Saul's resident priest, to be sent on missions, as called for, and Saul would supposedly pay him? But I was guessing. It all just brought back images: everything pointing toward Saul seemed to have *"Danger - Keep Out"* written on it.

We chatted a little, but Dorman was only interested in ogling young female flesh – plenty of it on show in The Botanics, known as a fetid haunt of certain thrill-seekers, though not usually during the daytime.

Naturally, Patricia was curious. I had mentioned Saul to her several times, but never in much detail, to keep my onward direction clear. It seemed that, when Saul was active in my affairs, life got very fraught, and now I wanted to be away from strife. When Patricia continued with her enquiries, putting her off with sweeping assurances only made her more curious. So, we came to a sort of agreement: if I did get a phone call from Dorman, or from Saul, and if Saul was coming back into my life, then at that time I would put Patricia fully in the picture. Otherwise, no need to have prolonged discussions about Crazy Horse.

The summer was wearing along gracefully when, one evening, Dorman called; said there had been delays due to Saul's health problems, and some other problems of Saul, which I probably knew about. This was vague and I was uneasy. As I read somewhere, Trouble always brings his brother. Still, Dorman said he felt sure that I would get a call very soon. I was quite excited.

Patricia liked life calm and level, and it struck me that, under her soothing influence, I too had become a bit calmer. But now the old juices were running again. Who knew what might happen? But whatever it was, I said to myself that it wouldn't be calm and level.

That night, I tried to give Patricia a fuller picture of Saul: his background as far as I knew it, his main characteristics and his relations with other people. I peppered my description with anecdotes, of which there were multitudes, and Patricia made a few sagacious comments. The one which stayed with me most was that Saul was someone going through life with a key part missing.

But, when the call came, two nights later, it was not from Saul, and it was not from Dorman.

12

"Hello, John. I bet you never guessed: it's Jane. Yes, Saul's aunt. I wish this was one of those new video calls, so I could see the astonishment on your face. Ha-ha. But that's unfair; you are a lovely man, and we got on so well, when you were kind enough to visit me.

"Well, John, I have a lot to tell you. The first thing is that, at last, they have let me go! Loads of conditions, on sheets of paper that I'm never going to read, but I'm out; I'm home. Not with Bert; I'm renting an apartment, here in Kelvingrove – very spacious; across the whole first level – nearly big enough for me to open a stately pleasure-dome!"

I managed to get a few remarks in here and there, but it was mostly a monologue. I did not mind; listening to her was a delight. She had a manner of speaking and a choice of phrase which is fast dying – at least in Glasgow.

"Now, John, I know my man's been in contact with you, so I know you have a lovely new lady-friend. And I know that you haven't been in touch with Saul for a while. There is a problem there which must be dealt with very soon, before it's too late: poor lad, he's just crumbling like a coffee meringue. Would you be able to visit me at all, John, so we could discuss the problem?"

As I listened to Jane, and knew this invitation was coming, I was thinking back over the last couple of years, and the various ways I'd tried to be kind to Saul. With Patricia, my life had taken on a new perspective, with new interests, and laughter was in my life a lot more. I asked myself what John the Baptist would do. Then I said yes to Jane's invitation.

She said the invitation extended to Patricia, too, but she would leave that up to me. The address she provided was familiar territory, and it was set for the next afternoon to have tea. She added that one or two others might be there.

The front door opened as I reached it, and there stood Dorman, in yet another guise: this time the formal dress of a butler or chief servant, or something. But his musical tones had not changed.

"Nice to see you, Mr. John. You're expected in that room across the hallway."

I strolled over, knocked and heard Jane's merry laugh. I went in and was amazed to see Saul, sitting across the room on a sofa, wearing a nice, lightweight suit, along with a pale shirt and rich tie. There were no sneakers on his feet now, but trendy blue-leather shoes by Camper. The light was not strong, yet he was away across a big room.

Strangely, Jane had not said a word since I came in. I stuttered: "Hi, Saul, you're looking good. Just shows you. I'd heard you were on the skids, but the rumours were all wrong, by the looks of it. So, what are you up to these days?"

The reply was in the wrong voice. I learned then what true

shock is really like; the voice was wrong because the man on the sofa was not Saul! From the middle of the room, my eyes now told me that. Yet, I could not figure it out. This was a dead ringer for my pal Saul – hair, nose, eyes, chin, build – but the speaking voice contradicted all other evidence. And, when he held out his right hand for a handshake, it was easy to see that the index and middle fingers were missing.

I stumbled backward a little, saw Jane sitting holding a glass of sherry, and gabbled something about what on Earth was going on; I heard myself even asking: "Is this the doppelganger?"

To my further surprise, I got an answer from Jane: "Yes, you might call it that in fun, but it's not entirely accurate. John, I want you to meet Peter Terry; he is the brother of your good friend Saul Terry. He is visiting me, and of course he is very keen to hear about his brother and, hopefully, to meet him. Isn't that so, Peter?"

His voice was deep and kind of rumbling. It had a soothing effect, and I felt my nerves relaxing and my brain slowing down. As he began to speak, part of my brain was really telling me I was listening to Saul – but Saul never in his life spoke like this: low, polite, slow and eloquent. As I came closer, I saw that the faces also differed slightly: whereas Saul was animated and forever twitching about, Peter's was a face of smooth, symmetrical slopes.

"Very pleased to make your acquaintance, John. I am still struggling to come to terms with this astonishing news. I do hope a great deal of good and joy will come of it. Aunt Jane tells me you are the man to help, John."

A ring on the bell brought Dorman in, with a couple of visitors: this time it was George and Jean, Jane's closest neighbours from her previous abode with Bert. A jolly pair. George was at once waltzing Jane around the table, while Jean plonked a bundle of presents on the sideboard, including Courvoisier brandy and Hendrick's gin. Introductions were resumed and Jane led us through to another room, where a table was set for afternoon tea; we were all told to take a seat. I sat next to Peter.

The place was buzzing, and even Dorman was grinning – not a pleasant sight – as the banter, and the sandwiches and cakes, flew around the company. I was glad to see that Dorman too had a place at the table, and was not some slave of Queen Jane. Jane explained, for my benefit and Peter's, that George and Jean were her closest friends, and had been her support during the rocky times with Bert, then the shoplifting crisis and its consequences. There was almost a party atmosphere.

After a while the pace slowed, and Jane asked would we like to hear a lovely true story. The first part of the story was hers, she insisted playfully, so she would tell that part – the preface, as she called it – then she would ask Peter to expand the story, with some details only he could know. The company gave full approval to this plan, and Jane began:

"I was only a few days into my freedom; less than a week out of the asylum... I had left my shadow behind in there, in chains; I had escaped! A miracle, because every one of them who had a say in my future was crazy… insane! I could tell them anything. I used to think that psychiatrists believed nothing a patient told them; now I know they believe absolutely anything they are told. It's a madhouse! Anyway, skipping along the Great Western Road, one afternoon last month, I saw a face I thought I recognized, on the other side of the street. I called out: 'Saul. Saul.' But he kept moving. So, I bawled out: 'Saul!' He must have heard me, but still he kept going. Then, he stopped at a bookshop and I darted across, nearly getting hit by a taxi, speeding off to some brothel or other. I placed myself bang in front of Saul, only to find that it was not Saul; it was Peter here. They do have differences up close, but from just a few yards away you might not tell which was who – as John here experienced, when he came in. Peter recognized me, I'm glad to say – very glad, because if he had not, I would almost certainly be back in a cell at the asylum. Peter was totally unruffled, looked at me steadily for a minute and said:

"'Aren't you my Aunt Jane, from long, long ago?'

"My heart leapt; he had recognized me! I had been used to seeing Saul from time to time, but never thought that his brother would come up out of the ground and stand in front of me, in a busy Glasgow Street.

"However, I now need to go back in time, to where we all started from. My parents had three of us girls – Barbara, Cora and myself – and we were brought up in our native village of Rockcliffe, a lovely little place on the Solway Firth. I was the youngest, Cora two years older, but Barbara was fourteen years older than me.

"In those days, it was common for gypsies to come travelling from village to village, throughout the borders; one of them once gave me a little bunch of primroses – I've never forgotten it. The other thing I recall, only distantly, was how strong and nimble their tongues were; they spoke the same language as us, but in some magical way, and they had words for things we only heard from them. And they sang and played tunes, which rambled just like they did. They cast a spell on my sister Barbara, and she fell for one of these gypsies; he seduced Barbara and she got pregnant. The gypsies moved on, as they do, and in nine months a son was born, to be named Saul.

"The gypsies like to live in cyclic patterns, and they returned a year later, when Saul was about three months old. Barbara panicked. Again she met the father, but she told him nothing about Saul; she was afraid they would snatch the baby and take him away with them. They resumed their passion and she got pregnant again. The caravans again moved off, and nine months later Peter was born.

"But, after the birth of Peter, the band of gypsies did not reappear. So, Barbara took Saul and a few belongings, and set off in pursuit of her lover and his travelling caravan. Peter was left in the care of my parents, who rather recklessly put it about that Cora was his mother. At first this worked a little, but soon Cora got very annoyed with this life imposed on her; she became very strict with Peter, who was only a little boy still; there were big fights in the house.

"At the age of eighteen, she announced that she'd had enough. She knew she had a vocation to the religious life, and she entered a convent of nuns as a novice; with that order she has remained. So,

I more or less looked after Peter, with the help of my lovely mum and dad. Peter went to a local school, and was nearing the time of moving to a secondary, when certain new things came into my own life. I won't go off on a tangent here about that – it would take forever – but I took off from the south and made a new life, in different parts of central and northern Scotland. I never saw Peter again, until that destined meeting the other week. So I really drop out of the story here… This might be a good time to ask Peter to pick up the trail from Solway.

"But first I think it is time for a wee dram, or something. That was lovely tea, and there's not a sandwich left – I thought for a terrible minute that Bert had got back in among us – but, good as it is, sometimes something stronger than tea is needed."

13

Peter stood up to remove his jacket. Same height as Saul, but trimmer and more wiry. To be honest, I knew he would tell us about his youth along the Solway, but I hoped he would also explain about his two missing fingers.

"My memories of my boyhood, down around the Firth, are not all good. Most of the memories are fuzzy, but I do recall being shouted at and punished – often unjustly – by my Aunt Cora, as I now know her. She was given a tough role, no question, and not given any choice in the matter, which is even worse. But she took her resentments out on me, and it was Aunt Jane here who many times saved me from a beating or a 'food suspension', as Cora liked to call it. When Cora left, I did actually leap for joy, though of course I did it privately, because I could not quite believe that she wasn't still around somewhere, watching me. When Aunt Jane left, I was upset, but I was also reaching a very new stage in my life, and so I was less preoccupied with things at home, who was going to feed me and so on. I was moving on.

"After school, I got accepted to enter the Royal Music Conservatoire Annexe, in Dumfries. Music was the true love of my grandfather's life. He genuinely sought out and absorbed the best of many kinds of music: jazz, bluegrass, skiffle, everything that came out of the rock'n'roll age, but also folk and traditional music, and some classical music. He had an ancient banjo he could pull a fair tune out of, and was quite adept on the mouth-organ. I often wondered if he was out of place on that farm in the south, with never a chance of any live musical performances at that time. The gypsies, when they called, would always put on one or two performances by night-fires, with thrilling melodies on the fiddles and rhythms of the boranns. Some gypsies endeared themselves to him less than others, of course. I enjoyed my degree course, got qualified and got a job teaching music, then a post back in the academy itself.

"I got married in Dumfries, to Karen – a bad decision on my part. We had a son, Edward, a real bonnie, wee lad. One day, when he was four years old, Karen and I were arguing and fighting about her drinking, as usual; it was early morning, but she had been drinking again. Karen had not realized that Edward was standing in the driveway behind the car, and in a moment of temper and fury, Karen let the brake off and reversed straight into Edward. He died right away. Three months later, Karen went away with an Edinburgh gangster – good riddance to both! But I had a breakdown and was hospitalized for… well, a long time.

"They were kind to me at the academy and, when I felt strong enough to return, they could not have been kinder. For a couple of years I had some contentment; I lived in a flat in Dumfries during the working week, and at weekends I always went down to the cottage in Rockcliffe, my grandparents having by now passed on. There was a lady in the Performing Arts department I had taken to, and was quietly hoping to get closer to, in time – though I was very hesitant, after what had gone before. I did start to see some signs of interest coming from her.

"All previous stages of my life had come to a bad end, and this one was to be no exception. I was tutoring a student by the name of Gary, who had to be reminded of the need to work hard and, above all, to practice. But he was lazy and he was devious; he needed to pass, and he decided it best to put pressure on me to get that pass. Mistaking me completely, because I was a single man and a music teacher, he offered me sexual rewards, which were utterly repugnant to me. When he realized his mistake, he changed his plan and tried to blackmail me, threatening to say I had molested him. I stood my ground and called his bluff. The truth was easily brought out and the student was immediately expelled; I thought that nightmare was also over. But not quite: two thugs hired by Gary followed me down to the cottage, and severed my index and middle-right fingers. All three were imprisoned and my professional career was finished.

"I'm sorry. I knew that would be difficult, but it had to be done. I feel a little shaky right now – Jane, could you put a little more brandy in there? Thanks. I'll be okay in a minute."

We were all silent for a few minutes. I was thinking it was like listening to an account of the *Book of Job*. But he was not finished yet; maybe there were more torments to come. Peter looked a little better, though said he would take a few minutes in the fresh air before continuing.

As he did so, we talked quietly. Jane told us how Peter had agreed to come and stay with her for a few days, to get reacquainted. That was not so hard. But telling Peter he had a brother was trickier; his response was strange: very lowkey, with no glorias or hallelujahs; maybe he hardly believed her.

Jane dealt with the situation equally calmly. It had been weeks since she had seen or spoken to Saul. She knew he was in decline, so she was cautious about being too definite as to his whereabouts. Luckily, Peter did not pester her for details. She considered that the misfortunes of his life had been such that he had built up a deep stoicism about any news, good or bad. Jane thought the best way would be to make her own enquiries as to where Saul was living, then ascertain whether Peter wanted to meet his brother. So far, he had still not indicated.

As we all heard, what a life he'd had! And, of course, Saul could be a ruffian. Maybe that's unfair, but he could be wild and impulsive, and Lord knew how he would respond to Peter. Probably do something crazy, like take him on a tour of the West End bars, to start with.

The lugubrious Father Dorman now spoke. He told us he knew where Saul was living, and it was not pleasant nor hopeful. He was all for brotherly love, as they'd expect, but this might end in calamity. I wondered at Dorman's gloominess, and not for the first time. I recalled Saul continually muttering how he'd keep an eye on Dorman.

I asked him: "Is Saul staying in the parish you're in, Father?"

"My parish? Sorry, no, no, no; I thought you knew: I'm not a priest. Being a priest is one of the roles Jane here likes me to play, and for that I have to dress correctly. I did once study for the priesthood – was even in a seminary for four years – so I know a fair bit about them, and you would be surprised how useful that can be. But it's only one of several ideas Jane has for me, and I love to play along. It's fun for her and she is worth it. I am, in all things, her humble servant."

Quite a speech. Jean and George smiled throughout, so I supposed they must be in on the joke – if a joke it was. Did Saul know? Did Peter know? Who knew what? It was all quite baffling. I recalled the image of Dorman drooling, sprawled like a gross sunflower in the Botanic Gardens.

Jane purred: "Mandor is my rock. 'Mandor' is what I sometimes call him… depending – don't I, my warrior?"

Dorman squirmed a little and smiled coyly.

"If I *were* a priest," (at this, he smiled at Jane) "I might put it like this: Saul is living where he has only limited access to the influence of good company." Mandor intoned this couplet so well that I almost found myself singing *"Amen"* in response.

14

Jane brought some focus to the question of the moment: "Right, John, I've given this much thought and I believe you'd be best to tell Saul what has happened, and to judge from his reactions what's to be done next. Neither of the brothers may be at all happy at the thought of meeting the other; we'll know a lot more once you've gone on this mission, John – and come back, of course."

This time I felt more resistant. I sensed a swamp bubbling away, not far in front of me, and I was being invited to try to navigate it. I was framing my refusal, when the door creaked and in came Peter. He looked tired. He came over and offered a double handshake – and my resistance was gone.

"Sorry, folks," he said, "I didn't manage to finish my story.

"So, anyway, after those terrible events I've told you about, by 2005 the whole matter was over. Despite everything, I managed to teach myself a little of how to play the fiddle, and I made a few friends down there in some of the hotels and bars, joining in with some jazz or traditional groups, a few nights a week. I took some university courses and have recently been asked to do some distance learning work with music students.

"Lastly, and I have very deliberately kept this 'til the end, I have been doing some work as a comedian, in some gigs around the North of England – nothing serious… ha-ha! Very deadpan. I had a companion, Sid, and we performed a little knockabout together; started as an interval act at music gigs – just fifteen minutes or so. It never got much longer than that, so there was no intention to develop the act into a full stage-show or anything. But, sadly, Sid's got dementia now and is out of reach, in a home.

"To a lot of you Glaswegians, my life might be really boring, but I'm content enough with it. I come up to Glasgow or Edinburgh quite often – well, every couple of months; I like second-hand and antique bookshops. That's how Jane saw me. And now I have a brother! It's all a bit overwhelming."

You couldn't say he sounded happy about the prospect of meeting his brother; maybe he was a little bit scared. I would have to bear that in mind, if I was to go on this mission as a mediator.

Jane announced that her friends' visit was not entirely a social one – there was a little business involved, too – so the four of them would be retiring for a little while to another room. Maybe I could entertain Peter; they would only be an hour, at the most. Then they sauntered off, bright and chuckling – even Dorman. To me, this seemed an obvious part of Jane's plan: to give me some time alone with Peter, to see what I might learn.

So, Peter and I talked. He was not cagey; he was quite open, and seemed a very trusting man. He still had several acquaintances in the south, and some female fans who liked his fiddling. He also wrote a little regular piece for the local paper, so he did not have financial worries. The cottage was a little isolated, and he had some concerns about being cut off but, considering the awful crises in his life, he was remarkably at peace. He drank sparkling water with lemon in it, and when he took a draught his face and even his head seemed to move around a little, as if some tectonic plates inside the skull were stirring. He saw me looking and laughed; the tectonic plates shifted a bit more. He chortled and said to me: "You can see already where my stage act begins and ends."

This was marvellous, and quite unexpected, that this polite and studious gentleman should transform instantly into a carnival act. He had me captivated, and he took advantage of the moment to ask:

"Well, does my brother Saul do anything like that?"

That opened things up for me to talk a bit about Saul, as I knew him and had known him. I filled in some of the school history, that of our paths crossing over the years, of the tensions in Saul's life, when I last saw him about a year ago, and about Saul's one-time obsession with meetings, and getting to as many of them as was possible. Peter nodded away and listened with interest, but offered little response that I could evaluate.

"He's usually at his best," I explained, "when he's in a bar called The Palace of Mirrors, over in Anniesland. He's at home there, though by no means a full-time attender. Outside of there, he can be nervy – agitated, even – and uncertain. I'm just trying to think if The Palace of Mirrors would be a suitable place for you to meet."

"I'm not fussy, John; to be fussy after all this time would be ridiculous. I'm not much of a drinker, but I'm not uneasy in pubs; I play in them quite a lot. However, Aunt Jane might have other ideas, don't you think?"

I explained to Peter that the consensus was that I should inform Saul about his brother, and pave the way for a meeting, if mutually desired. Peter seemed to be aware of this arrangement, so I suggested we defer any further decisions until I had seen Saul.

And, that being the case, we agreed to go in search of our hostess and her friends. We heard their chatter in a faraway room and proceeded there. Knocking and entering, we saw Jane and George at one table, and Jean and Dorman at another; on each table was the skeleton of a jigsaw puzzle. They were working in teams at the tasks, and throwing banter back and forth as they put a piece in place. On the walls of the room were about a dozen completed jigsaws, which had been placed on red vinyl and covered in clear Perspex. They were not the usual awful studies of kittens or puppies, or a stream flowing past a thatched cottage; one was of a castle constructed of musical instruments; another was a mock-horror Hallowe'en scene; another was a mystifying picture of a magician's study. Peter and I strolled around as if we were in some gothic gallery, even as the next exhibits were being created. Peter whispered that he had heard how doing jigsaw puzzles had two great benefits: first, they could bring a spiritual balance; and second, they gave the brain practice in specific problem-solving, in which only one solution was possible, and you had to keep going until you found it – there were no compromise solutions.

"Look, lads," said George, presumably addressing myself and Peter, "there's another table like these; maybe next time you could get started on a puzzle together."

I had no wish to be rude, but George's permanent grin, all gnashers flashing, gave me a spooky recall of that old horror film *Rosemary's Baby*. Instead, I said: "I really look forward to that… eventually. But I have got my mind on this other task right now. Listen, wouldn't it be fine to think of Saul and Peter occupying that table some time?"

That drew murmurs of approval, and provided a chance for me to announce that I had to be somewhere quite soon. I expected Jane to say that Dorman would call me, and give me directions to Saul; instead, Dorman took out a sheet of paper with an address written on it: *"129 James Street, Helensburgh."*

Dorman intoned: "You can go any time, any day; Saul will be there. But, please let Jane know when you are going and when you've returned."

15

I had not been down to Helensburgh for about 25 years.

A regular train runs from Glasgow, and in 45 minutes I was on the pavement looking for the fabulous Break No Record shop, which had once stood across from the station, a beacon of delight. But no more; it was now a nail bar. It was the same along the waterfront: mobile phone repairs, charity shops, Kingburger… the old, elegant tearooms and fifties-style cafés were long gone. By the pier, the most dreadfully rundown showground – including a mini rollercoaster ride, which was partly held together with duct-tape – plunged visitors into a deep depression, especially those who could remember how lovely this little town once was. It did not bode well for my visit. Saul's address was halfway up a street which ran down into the scrapyard operating at the end of the waterfront.

I had gone down early to avoid any rush, and I now sat on a bench and looked across to Greenock, on the far bank of the Clyde, at its widest at just this point. To go farther west than Helensburgh is to enter Argyle, and sense that you are leaving urban Scotland behind. Maybe that was in Saul's thinking, though this was only a guess. The weather was mild, but summer had packed up for the year.

After sitting for a while, I knew I could not postpone the

moment any longer.

"Who in hell is that?" was the guttural call as I arrived, three flights up, in front of flat 3/1. My nerves jangled, but I knew the voice and I knew the tone.

I went in, past two bedrooms on the right, a bathroom on the left and into a living room, with several lamps dotted around the floor; no overhead lights, but a lot of carpet and cushions. The air was quite pungent.

From the doorway, I looked down at Saul, seated cross-legged and rattling some dice in his hand. We might have been in Tehran. I moved closer to him and sat down on a footstool – only then did he look up. He seemed puzzled. Then I remembered about his weakening eyesight.

"Saul, it's John."

He put the dice in a little jade cup, as he tried to focus on me. "Hiya, John. Glad you came, cos I have been going over a few ideas, and it kept coming to me that you'd be the man to help me with some of these."

Even if his sight was fading, the brain had not changed much.

"Helping you was getting difficult, Saul. But I would have always come; why didn't you ever phone?"

"Hate phones; don't get me started on phones! People walking about the streets seeing nothing, phones in front of their eyes... They walk into lampposts, walk into other people, then get up and start looking at their phones again. Lunacy. I have no phone."

"I heard your sight was getting worse. But Saul, surely a bit more light in here would be a good idea? These lamps are nice –

they create a mystical sort of atmosphere – but you need to see; you need some overhead lighting."

"I can adjust. I don't read a lot, though I do try to get some thoughts written down on paper. Been thinking about the east a lot. Were we ever there?"

"Where?"

"The east. Did we ever go east?"

"You mean the east end of Glasgow? Shettleston and thereabouts?"

"Don't be funny, John. Leave the jokes to me; you were always better as the straight man. We'll talk about the east later. Would you like some tea?"

He had teamaking things right beside him, on a kind of single-filament heater. So, we drank tea, which was certainly not Tetley's, with sugar but no milk. And we seemed to get a little calmer.

I reminded myself that I could not leave here without completing my mission. I was wondering how blunt I should be – how frank and how inquisitive about Saul – but he helped me out.

"You couldn't say that Helensburgh has everything a man needs, John, but it's not bad for me just now. I've been here for several weeks, I think. Glasgow was getting a wee bit dangerous. I was drinking too much, that Palace crowd were too close and too convenient, and things from the past were catching up on me – people, too. You remember Lydia; she was with us that night of the rammy? Well, she started to haunt me. It got bad; I couldn't shake her off. She was besotted with me, despite the age gap. She wanted us to get together and I said no. The breakup was bad – very bad. If you can be patient, I'll try to explain but, believe me, it's tangled.

"Well, I once told you about how my interest in meetings started, and that was how it stayed for a long time. But then, things changed: the reason I went to so many meetings became to find runners for Benny and his partner, Sandy. You know how the gangs operate in Glasgow: somebody gets shot in a car, or from a car, and it's all over the tabloids for a day or two. These gangs – the Conways and the Shorts – are well known. But there are other gangs, who are much more invisible; they do everything they can to avoid notice and publicity. Benny and Sandy are gang members; I don't know what rank they are, or if the gang even has a name. Anyway, they got me to do a quiet job of weapons delivery: just three pistols and some ammo. I was broke at the time and the money was very tempting. Afterward, they told me that the package also contained a load of crack cocaine, and that they had video evidence of me with the stuff; I was under their control. I was told I would be released from that control, or promoted out of it, when I had recruited five runners. It was made clear that the runners had to be poor, quiet, steady, sensible and fearless – and, above all, anonymous. They said that obviously I did not meet the requirements as a runner, that I was far too loud, so I would have to do some recruiting. They'd heard that I went to a lot of meetings – all kinds of meetings – and that was just what they were looking for; I was told many recruits could be found at these meetings, which had no connection whatever to organized crime. That was exactly the kind of recruit Benny was after. So, I went to meetings… as you well know.

"As I tell you this, I feel totally idiotic, but it is the way it worked. I had found three recruits and was a bundle of nerves, day and night, waiting for the police to turn up. My fourth recruit was Lydia."

"Lydia from the purple-dye trade?"

"Yes – that was code, of course. It was at a meeting for the Seamen's Mission volunteers. As I said, she fell for me and I fancied her, but she was a perfect recruit for Benny, and she agreed right away. So, now I needed one more recruit to get out. I was getting desperate, dragging this ball and chain everywhere.

"Then, I got introduced to her younger sister Agnes, a sweet girl, very innocent-looking. Jocky had to have her, and that was my contract fulfilled; I could go. But I knew I had made a mistake. Agnes got caught in possession of some guns and dope; she's in jail now, awaiting trial. It keeps getting postponed, because they want to find the bigger fish, knowing full well that Agnes is only a tiddler.

"I got out of town and Dorman found this place for me; particularly important to lie low for a bit, and Dorman said Helensburgh was as low as you'll get. He was right; nobody comes here now. It used to be very popular, too; now it's a ghost town. But it's not permanent – no chance. Not time yet to make a move, though.

"What about you? How ya been?"

I told him about Patricia, and how we seemed to be good

influences on one another. I also told him I'd cut back on visits to The Palace and, with my new companion on the scene, I no longer missed the pub as much as I would have done. This was a little dishonest, because I was still a regular, but I was trying to avoid giving Saul the idea he should get back to his old ways. His old haunts, like The Palace, would be the easiest of targets for anyone out to harm Saul. I was tempted to ask a lot of nosy questions about his gang experiences, but instead changed tack altogether.

"I did bump into your old pal Father Dorman, about ten days ago. Strolling in the Botanics with Patricia, I saw this guy I recognized – not by his priestly clothes, though; he was dressed like a summer tourist from the sticks: colour on legs. And he couldn't keep his eyes off the women! You still in touch with him?"

"Yep, still in touch. I'm at the very edge of the known world here, John. I may be in seclusion, but I still need my antenna – otherwise, how am I to know when danger is approaching? So, of course the reverend is in touch."

"By phone? I thought you'd no phone."

"By phone, yes, but not to me; he phones the guy who owns the chippy down at the corner, and Aldo comes up and passes on any message. It's usually kinda coded, but not too tricky to grasp. Aldo's an interesting guy, by the way; got a bit of history himself. And, you've guessed it, John: Aldo's not his real name, but it'll do for now.

"Need to get up for a minute. Can you help me?"

I had to pull him upright by the arms. He was lighter than he used to be, and the limp more noticeable as he made for the bathroom.

I saw a few photos propped around the place. One caught my attention because it was in a beautiful, dark frame, crafted with great skill: it was a photo of a woman of around thirty. She didn't quite look like Jane, though there was a resemblance; maybe it was Cora, Jane's sister, though she was not dressed like any traditional nun.

Saul said: "You must be hungry. Normally I would have cooked something nice for you, for lunch, but I didn't know you was coming. So, I suggest we go along to Aldo's, have a nice pizza or a Bolognese? Not what you'll be used to, but it's fresh and tasty. C'mon."

He hobbled out in his white, collarless shirt, his mid-length pantaloons and some jazzy-looking bronze slippers. He left the door ajar. I looked at him in surprise.

"It's okay," he said, "nobody comes here. I got fed up with forgetting to take my keys, so I just decided to go without locking it. It's paid off up to now. C'mon, you must be starving."

So much for paranoia, I thought.

He went slowly down the five flights, and I wondered how on Earth he could get back up. In James Street, he nodded to a few acquaintances, and got a very friendly greeting when he stepped inside the chippy.

16

"This is John," he said, "an old school pal come to visit; I've brought him along to taste your food – where else would I go? – so don't let me down!"

He was more his old self in a place like this. It had been an estate agent's business, when people could buy houses. The chippy was extended to include a few chairs and small tables, but it was basically a takeaway. At the counter, you helped yourself to salt, vinegar and tomato sauce. I went for an old-fashioned fish tea: haddock, chips, peas, bread and butter, and a pot of tea. Saul had a large pizza, decorated with several species. Saul mentioned how Italians always seemed good at turning their place into a family business; family was always part of their culture. He had met Aldo's three brothers, who took turns helping at the counter and the tables. Three of them looked alike, and all their names ended in o – Antonio, Riccardo and Alfredo – so I called them "The Three Oh Boys", but not one of them had heard of Buddy Holly.

I saw how Saul enjoyed his pizza, eating with open relish, and wondered if he ate regularly; he had lost weight. But his eyesight was a little stronger in daylight. I suppose I was building up an assessment of him, which I could pass on to Peter.

Saul did not offer to pay for the meal, nor to share the bill, so I left him still wolfing away, and went over to talk to Aldo.

"Such a nice man, Saul; sometimes very funny," Aldo told me. "Have to be careful, though; he can explode suddenly. He come in to talk sometimes and sit down, but no buy anything. I tell him I love him like a brother, but I gotta run this business, too; I tell him chips no grow on trees. He say: 'Well, you learn something new every day.' He can be good fun, but sometimes his jokes about my brothers no nice – too personal. He not got too much sense, your pal. Maybe you should help him. He never do any work? I think work would be good for him."

"He stopped working some time ago," I replied. "It was complicated. He has always had some problems."

"Well, yes, we all got problems. I got a problem if somebody cannot come in to eat, because Saul is sitting there and no buying anything. Do you know if he has no money?"

"I'll try and find out more about that, Aldo. This is the first time we've met for ages, so I don't know yet what his circumstances really are."

"Okay, okay. Listen, this meal is on me, this time; free for you and Saul. But he has to start paying. He can be very funny; make us all laugh. Maybe he should be a *comico*: a comedian."

After lunch, we walked along the promenade and crossed to sit on a bench facing the water. Our chat and banter showed no sign of abating, so I realized I was just going to have to grasp this nettle; waiting for the perfect moment was never going to work.

"Saul, I was looking at your photos in the flat. That one looks like Jane, but I suppose it might be the other one… Cora?"

"That's my mother, Barbara."

"I remember you saying in class one day that your mother was dead; that you had no one."

"That's right: she died when I was about eight or nine, not sure. Life was different then. We were all travellers; we lived in wagons. There were hundreds of us when we'd meet at great fairs, at Appleby or Kirkby Lonsdale. My mother and I were part of a big family – bigger than those Italian families we were talking about. I had no idea who I was, except I had a name – Saul – and I was one of the travelling people. One day, I was feeding the dogs, when a man called Harman took me aside and told me my mother had died. I have a vague picture of the funeral, the firelight and the singing, but I had no great feelings otherwise. Then, we just sort of travelled on. With the weather in this country, you have to be tough to be a traveller.

"Then, one day, when I'd be about eleven, a man and a woman came and talked to Harman and the others. They talked nearly all day. I was taken to Glasgow, put in a home for boys, and put to schooling. Five years later, I was sitting beside you in a class, studying Higher Latin.

"After school, somehow I got into the piping business, and lasted a long time with them; I even won some awards. But they didn't care about awards; they wanted reliability, and I couldn't give them that. Now I get money occasionally, from odd work playing the bagpipes. Did Aldo tell you I should get a job? He's always harping on about that. But, what is there?"

"Aldo also said that you're a comic. Maybe you should try the stage; older people are always needed. I know one or two guys at the Citizens, and even at Oran Mor."

"Listen, John, I know you've still to tell me why you've really come down here – I just hope it's not to help me get a job telling jokes in Oran Mor."

So, here goes, I said to myself.

"No, Saul, it's a family matter. Saul, you're not alone; you have a brother. He's alive and his name is Peter: Peter Terry. I've met him."

Saul was very still; for once, no part of him was in motion. I thought he was going to break down in tears. He started shaking his head a lot, then he was moving his lips in some silent monologue. He stared at the water and said to me: "It's not possible that you are kidding in any way? Or that you've made a mistake?"

"If you see Peter, you will have no doubts about the answer to that question."

"He's like me? He looks like me?"

"Yes, he does. Not identical, though."

"Of course he's not identical; the doppelganger need not be identical – that's a popular fantasy."

"You're still hunting for this doppelganger?"

"Not any longer; we've found him! Wasn't I right? People thought I was mad. *You* did. *I* nearly did! I knew it! My god, now I'm terrified; look at the state of me. Be honest, John: I hope he doesn't look like the way I look."

I gripped his arms and shook them. "He is not a doppelganger.

I met him the day before yesterday, in your Aunt Jane's house. Jane deserves all the credit here; she found him."

"Found him? Whaddya mean, found him? You mean he was lost, or what?"

"No, she saw him on Great Western Road, standing at that bookshop you know only too well."

"How long ago was this?"

"Just recently; days, I think."

"Will I like him?"

"Yes, I'm sure you will, although I only met him once, quite briefly. We talked some. He doesn't talk like you, though."

"What's that mean?"

"He's calm, maybe even slow. Not excitable."

"Ah, I see! So, Aunt Jane has sent you along on a mission to see if the brothers, long lost to each other, can meet without an explosion?"

"I can't see Peter doing any exploding."

"So, I expect you've come with a whole file of information for me. Are you gonna show me it? Is it a long story? A sad story?"

By now, we were up and walking along the front, and I gathered my ideas to give Saul as clear a version as I could put together. I expected interruptions at every turn, but they were quite rare; he did a lot of headshaking and muttering to himself, but he did not break the flow of my account. I left out a lot of details, some of which I was still confused or ignorant about, and I knew they would best come later. I told him that Peter was a year younger, and that he was left with his grandmother, when Barbara left home to make a life elsewhere. That Peter was put to school in St, Joseph's, Dumfries, a Catholic school run by the Marist Brothers. Still living down in the borders, he went on to study at the Conservatoire Annexe, then did music teaching for a while, before an accident put an end to that. I explained that he'd had a settled and comfortable life for some years now, and that he came up to Glasgow occasionally, to visit antique bookshops. Jane herself hadn't seen him since he was about eleven or twelve, because she left home in the borders to find a more exciting life in Glasgow, yet they recognized each other. From that moment, Jane saw the chance of reuniting two long-separated brothers.

"Are they expecting you to tell me to pack a kitbag, and get bundled onto the train with you tonight? Because that's not going to happen, I'm afraid."

By this time, we were back at the stairs to his flat. The climb took him a while, and the talking could not resume until he was sitting on his cushions.

"There's whisky and brandy in that cupboard; whichever you like. We should surely drink to something." He splashed a dollop of Johnny Walker into the glasses and proposed: "Here's to Saint Peter; let's hope he has the keys to the Kingdom."

I was starting to feel cautiously hopeful: so far, it was a start which could be built on. Maybe that was why I skipped all references to the disasters in Peter's life: the blackmail, the mutilation, the death of his son… My idea was that, if Saul met Peter, a chemistry would come into play, which would pave the way for them to get close and share their histories. But I did tell

Saul a fair amount of what Peter looked like, talked like, some of his mannerisms and some of his interesting characteristics.

"Do you not think it's strange, even uncanny, that we never met or knew about one another? Did you say I was one year old when he was born? I have absolutely no memory of that, but I suppose that's not unusual."

"Everything's strange – but you know that. What do you think? Are you ready for meeting Peter? I'm sure it can be easily arranged. I mean, would you like a meeting to take place down here, instead?"

Saul laughed a genuine laugh of amusement. "You kidding? Among these pillows and lanterns? Anyway, you're rushing me a little. Tell me this straight out: does he want to meet me? And, if he does meet me, will he be shocked or delighted?"

Saul's caginess, wanting to play around the edges of this for the moment, had a subtle affinity with Peter's equally uncommitted response to the big news. They were brothers, after all, for all the different kinds of foliage life had grown on them.

"Yes, he does want to meet you, even after I told him in detail what a scoundrel you are. Just kidding. He made it clear, in his own way, that he wants to meet you. Shocked? He could be; I suppose that depends on which Saul turns up at the meeting. Remember how little I know him. If you want more time to consider it, fair enough, but it would mean you agreeing to get a phone and learning how to use it; the Aldo connection is just not going to be enough for business like this. Give it some thought. And go easy on that whisky. I'll be back in twenty minutes."

I got a simple phone for him in a local shop, and was back in less than fifteen. He was not drinking, and he did seem to be thinking.

"Now, pay attention," I said, and gave him a tutorial on basic use of the phone. He grasped it all immediately, making me wonder if he'd had a phone all along. I put my and Jane's numbers in the phone's contacts. He said that he already knew Dorman's, and I didn't put a number for Peter in because his brother didn't have one, either; maybe he too was a phonophobe.

"I'll be in touch soon. Please let me know right away if you have to leave here."

On the train up to Glasgow, I called Jane and gave her a positive report; I omitted all references to gangs and gun running. Jane had some link to Lydia, so maybe she already knew more than I did. She was thrilled, in her nutty kind of way, full of thanks and excitement about the prospects for us all. It made me reflect that, in an odd way, a strange little family was growing here.

And, sure enough, a week later she called to invite me to a little get together at her place. Before I asked, she added that Dorman would be conveying Saul to the gathering.

17

I could hear the tinkle of the "Goldberg Variations", as I arrived at the open door of Jane's flat. I knocked loudly and strolled in, as Jane's voice called:

"That you, John? The jigsaw room!"

The walls were still covered in jigsaws, but the centre of the room was now occupied by a large dining table with eight places; six of them were already occupied. There were two empty seats at the end farthest from Jane, and I chose one next to Dorman, facing across to Peter and Saul. Closer to Jane were Jean and George. Two ladies of different ages, but wearing the same maid's uniform, were standing in a corner – both smiled as I moved across the front of them. I was thinking: *Who is this Jane, really?*

The younger server came over and poured me a rather bitter aperitif. When I had taken a sip, there was silence. I glanced at my watch: I was not late, but I felt as if I was holding up proceedings. Just as I was about to crack a little jokey icebreaker, Dorman said:

"Please bow your heads and we will pray."

Finally, after this eloquent little grace, the bubble burst and everybody was chattering at once. Of course, I could not wait to find out how the great summit meeting of the Terrys had gone. But, looking across the table at them, I saw that I need have no fear: Peter was grasping Saul's arm and whispering into his ear; Saul's eyes were wide with wonder. It was a marvel.

Everyone at the table was a talker, but we all stopped nattering whenever Peter and Saul got into some animated subject. Their acquaintance was in its first bloom, and they were continually recalling things to pass on. They were equally fascinated by Saul's years travelling around the south with the gypsies, perhaps at times coming close to Peter without knowing. Peter could use his detailed knowledge of the Solway country to connect to memories Saul had of being at a fair, or in a village, entertaining or learning how to tell fortunes. Their comparisons showed that Saul must have travelled through Rockcliffe more than once, his mother keeping a low profile inside their wagon. How strange, too, they realized, that Joseph's College, Dumfries and St. Mungo's Academy, Glasgow were both run by the same religious order: the Marist Brothers. Although the overall ethos of each school was the same, the brothers had benefitted differently from their experiences under the strict discipline of the Marists. Peter teased Saul as being driven wild and crazy by his time in the Academy (Saul must have been open and honest about some of his later follies), but Saul was kinder to his brother, only allowing himself to tell the company in jest about how excited Peter had been the other day, to see colour television for the first time. At another point, while tucking into some sole, Peter was saying just how much he loved fish, and that he ate it a lot; Saul added that it was a pity he had to go and catch it for himself every day, as if he thought Solway was like somewhere deep in South America.

It was at this point that Peter revisited the episode of how his fingers were lost. He had us in a spell, as he unfolded the various stages of that ordeal.

He ended with some remarks about the Conservatoire Annexe, which he'd sadly had to part from. He had found out that, before its present use, the building had been The Crichton Institute for Lunatics. He suggested a doctoral thesis which might repay interest: a history of the close relation between music and madness. This Peter fellow was getting remarkably interesting to know.

The meal was well advanced, when Jane tinkled her spoon and stood up. "This will be the one and only speech:

"My nephews have been here for three days – one from the south and one from the west. Only I was present when they finally met; it was a meeting of joy and love and astonishment. And also, I should add, of promise! Not to mention plans – you'll hear about those in due course. Both boys were nervously terrified of this reunion yet, from the instant their eyes met, there was a recognition; I might call it an epiphany! I'm getting emotional already.

"Anyway, why don't we, when we've finished, go round to the sitting room and talk about the past and the future? But, just before we do, can I ask you to show a little appreciation for the excellent service provided by our two lovely girls, Francoise and Eleanor."

We applauded, for they had indeed added some spice and glamour to their faultless serving. In the sitting room, Jane added that they were a delight in many ways, and indeed that they offered quite a variety of services; here she looked at Saul, for some reason. He joined his hands as if in prayer, and raised his eyes to Heaven.

"The girls can be reached at a number I have; you need only ask."

In the sitting room, I was talking to Dorman and George about the present state of popular music, but the discussion was ragged from the start. Dorman seemed to want to include Frank Sinatra and Perry Como as modern, while George had never heard of Ed Sheeran. I was quite relieved when Peter called for attention.

"As you can imagine, Saul and I have been yakking non-stop for nearly three days. I find him to be a very amusing man; very witty. But, more interesting to me was that people seem to chuckle at Saul very easily, even before he says anything; he's a conduit for laughter. I am a bit like that, too. Now I know you're all saying: 'What?!' Well, I was telling Saul about my little stage act: a comic routine I used to do, in places around Galloway. Places like Castle Douglas and Dalbeattie: never-heard-of backwaters, but great for local entertainment. My partner's well out of the game now, his mind nearly gone, but yesterday I had a thought, and I put it to Saul: how about becoming my stage partner, as well as my brother? In fact, as brothers, we might have a little added glitz. So, yesterday for a while, when Jane was busy organizing this party, Saul and I did a little practising – or, at least, I showed him a kind of sketch we used to do: lots of miming and a little choreography; very little speech, and the occasional burst of a line or two of song—"

"Shall we show them what we've been trying, Peter?"

"No, no, Saul; too early! We're not even at rehearsals, yet. I don't think we even know yet where we're going to be staying. All this excitement and revelation has made poor old Rockcliffe fade into the background, but that'll change; I have some things to do down there, so I'll be heading back quite soon. It sounds a bit stupid to say it, but we've agreed to stay in touch. Ha-ha-ha."

"Peter, you were keen to see where I was living in Helensburgh. It's okay for me, but it's not up to much; it was never going to be my permanent residence, anyway, so it'll not be a lot of trouble for me to move – I've moved a lot, John can tell you. Of course, the nearer we can be to one another the better."

Jean and George had a proposition they thought Saul might like, and they arranged to talk to him separately about it. Jane looked thoughtful and almost sad, which was most unlike her. Perhaps she saw that the present camaraderie wouldn't last. I wondered if she rather wanted Peter and Saul to move into her apartments; there was plenty of room. This was maybe not to her liking – and, of course, quite likely not to the liking of the brothers, either; you get used to living single and, as life goes on, it gets harder to consider sharing your space permanently.

Patricia and I still lived separately, though within walking distance of each other. She doesn't come into this story a lot, because at that time she had a sister in Florida who was ill, and she decided to go back and spend some time with her. That gave me more leeway to deal with Saul, of course, but throughout that period I often wished Patricia was nearer, to give me advice and counsel – especially now that Peter was on the scene.

I was in the kitchen, rinsing a couple of glasses (the serving maids had disappeared into thin air) when Jane came in. She was not sad at all, but glowing.

"Oh, John, what a sight it was when they met! Peter was very nervous all morning and getting worse – even shaking. He had two sherries at noon, just before Saul arrived. I wondered if they were going to start circling each other, like two jungle cats. Then they hugged. Twice they each spoke at the same time and had to start again, amid roars of laughter. It was plain sailing from then."

"You know, Jane, this is bound to go well. I was thinking of their births, only a year apart; nature couldn't get them much closer. And, in almost identical circumstances as infants. After that, of course, life's been pepper and salt for both."

Jane gripped my hand. "You're so right; that's them: Peter and Saul… Pepper and Salt!"

18

Saul, Peter and I were having lunch in Bernini's, in the West End. It was three weeks since the reunion.

Peter had been down home and back again several times, and was hopeful that his discussions with his lawyer would go well. He had decisions to make about his cottage, and was still wondering about the best next move. I had no idea about his financial status, otherwise I might have advised him to retain the cottage for breaks and find a nice apartment in Glasgow. Unlike Saul, Peter was a man amenable to advice. I held back but stayed alert, in case Saul came in with any hairbrained advice of his own.

Saul was excited and clearly had news to tell us.

"Guess where I'm off to Monday morning. To an interview, that's where, over on the south side." He grinned at us like a cash register, waiting for us to beg for details.

"Remember George, Jane's pal? He's filed a claim for me and it could turn out to be a strike; a goldmine! It's a job with accommodation attached – in Cardonald, just through the Clyde Tunnel. It's in the bag, I think. But, just in case I slip up or something goes wrong, I'm not getting overconfident and blabbing about it 'til I know for sure. But I'm really jumping! And it's so funny; when you hear the details you will laugh, both of you."

My antennae beeped at the message that Saul was really

jumping; bound to be bad news for somebody!

But, across the afternoon it was mostly good vibes I was picking up. The brothers were strongly in touch, but nothing was being forced or overdone, and they were taking enough time to make important decisions. I would assume that by now Saul had overcome his phobia and phoned Peter regularly.

I asked how the comedy routine was coming along. They were enthusiastic, but reserved about its future. It needed endless rehearsing, even though it was more a mime than anything else. Saul said it reminded him of some of the great little routines Laurel and Hardy performed to perfection. Peter spoke with great love of one of these: a film called *Way Out West*, in which the duo performs this hilarious little dance to the fiddles and banjos of the soundtrack, with those inimitable smiles on their faces. Peter referred to this as the gold standard, and said they were never aiming for anything so high; it was just an ideal.

Anyway, it had been delayed a little, because Saul was having a little problem…

"Jesus, these dreams!" Saul told us. "They're driving me mad. I need to share this. Last night, I had a dream where I was riding a horse, going along easily at a gentle pace, feeling proud and risen in the world. But then the horse slowed and moved its head from side to side, as if looking for something. We were at a sort of golf course; a long, smooth lawn of grass flanked by forest on each side. Then, out of the left side came three other horses— Don't laugh, Peter; this isn't a joke; these weren't the Four Horsemen of the Whatdyecallit. The four horses started to talk among themselves; I did not know the language… well, of course. But, somehow I was able to pick up scraps of sense and meaning; something about why was my horse allowing people to sit on him and ride him around; wasn't he ashamed? They were abusing my horse for not being savage and free, and all that stuff.

"But my horse wasn't fazed at all. He was reminding them of an ancient covenant between man and horse, where the horses had offered their service to humans, to help them progress, back at the dawn of the human race. And, they should remember that a time was coming when horse and man would need each other again: when all this electronic baloney blew itself to smithereens, and we were back with the plough and the hoe.

"The visiting horses came closer and seemed threatening, but my horse reared up fully to intimidate them, and I came flying back off the horse, landing in a swamp next to the forest. I was sinking in the mud then, and I could see no horses – no one. Then I hit the floor of my bedroom. I've been having this dream, or versions of it, nearly every night this week."

Not knowing whether Saul had told his brother about the ride to Dumbarton and Saul's fall from grace, I held back.

Saul seemed to have his mind fixed on the future, rather than the past, for he said: "I wish I still knew that woman… what was her name? Delia, or something like that? She was a fortune-teller; a genuine seer, who could tell the future. I got to know her back when I was staying with Big Bertha. Bertha had some awful psychic troubles. Her hobby was throwing big things; she once threw a table at me! That was when I bailed out. But, I heard later that Delia did bring some peace of spirit to Big Bertha; brought her some peace and rest."

Peter was looking at Saul in some wonder. He said: "You must have come across some fortune tellers in your young days, so I suppose you might know if she was a true mystical seer. But maybe you don't remember much about that?"

"Only a little, and not in detail. Travellers are all expected learn some of the art of 'dukkerin'', I think they call it. I think a lot of our fortune tellers were fake; for them it was a trade to learn, to make some money from the 'gorgers' – you lot, that is. But there are two faces, which I can still visualize. At the time, I knew they had great powers; things did come true – though I was just a boy, so I might have been easily fooled. I don't believe in psychiatry, or I might try it."

"Maybe too late for psychiatrists, anyway; maybe it's an exorcist you need."

We stared at Peter, but he seemed serious.

"Maybe the reason that comes to mind is from an interesting conversation I had with Dorman, just a few days ago: he was telling me about his life, and we were discussing his days in the seminary. He left there before taking major orders, but he had still received the four minor orders of porter, lector, acolyte and exorcist. It was an astonishing fact. But, of course, there is a long, long way between receiving the order and carrying out an exorcism. Dorman told me that there is an active exorcist in the Glasgow archdiocese – a modest, lowly man, not particularly learned, but full of deep humility and stillness. Dorman said he worked away quietly as a priest, in one of the parishes in Glasgow. Nobody but the archbishop knew that, from time to time, this priest was called on to carry out an exorcism. Maybe we can find a way for you to reach him, if things get really worse."

I could see Saul regarding his new brother with mixed feelings: respect, surprise and maybe fear.

Jane turned up at 3.30, as arranged, to collect Peter.

Oh-ho, I thought, *no Dorman? What's this?* But I was off the mark; Jane told us Mandor was painting her kitchen, and wanted to do it all in one shift, so that the paint would dry evenly.

"Aunt Jane, you are lucky to have such a willing slave," said Saul, and it was hard to know what the tone of that was intended to be. I had never heard him once express anything near sympathy for Dorman, for all the good deeds that saintly impostor performed. Jane ignored him, except for the sweetest of smiles, which she cast about us as a benediction.

Saul and I stayed on for a bit in the restaurant. He told me a pal by the name of Jocky was away from home for a while – which could have meant a lot of things, but Saul didn't say what. Jocky had asked Saul if he would look after his place for a few weeks, which suited Saul very well, of course, for he was tiring of living in the Casbah in Helensburgh.

Saul had benefitted from the influences of Peter, but the old Saul was still in charge. The danger, as I saw it then, was that Saul would start to influence Peter, and that would not necessarily be for the better. I seemed to have spent years awaiting the conversion of Saul, though to what I did not know. I kept expecting him to have a moment of startling self-discovery – I did not know why I had this expectation.

Something was bothering Saul, and not just the dreams. We got to it when he asked: "Bet you can guess what question Peter has been putting to me?"

I hadn't a clue.

"He's been saying how he has made a number of journeys up to Glasgow, and I've never once even mentioned going down to visit him in Rockcliffe. He loves the journeys – he says they're what his life has been lacking – but he explained that he has a heart condition, and at a recent check-up his doctor advised him to slow down just a little. This, of course, makes it difficult for me to say no; I think I will have to make that visit to Rockcliffe."

"Why wouldn't you? It's in Solway, not Siam. Look how you used to be forever on the go, travelling everywhere to those meetings. Travelling's in your blood."

"Yes, but that was a different thing, and those meetings were nearly all around this area. Maybe you're forgetting where I came from?"

"Well, isn't that the whole point? You'd be visiting your home, your birthplace."

He was nervous about all of this, and I guessed from experience that, in his own time, he would tell me why.

"He looks quite like me, I know; can't deny it. But the life he's led, the way he's dealt with terrible misfortunes, that's nothing like me; it's just too opposite of me. That's why I'm tempted to go back to my original idea."

"Which is what?"

"Well, you know… he's my doppelganger, not my brother. Up here I feel safe enough, but down there in the forest, there's no telling; the doppelganger is often malevolent."

"Whoa, whoa! Peter has been eating with us; you've been spending a lot of time getting to know him! This doppelganger stuff has to stop! I hope you never mentioned it to Peter."

"Nah. Anyway, it would be dangerous to mention it to his face; could give the game away, I mean. Some things you keep well up your sleeve."

"Saul, I swear, I am walking out of here unless you tell me you recognize Peter as your long-lost brother, and you are going to get to know him."

"I'll have to think about this. Over these few weeks it's been great, talking for ages with Peter. He is so keen, naturally, for me to tell him all about our mother. I feel bad, because I can only remember brief snatches of things: moments, faces, bits of trouble... I've given him a pretty good idea of what she looked like, and how she spoke rather quickly – a bit like a bird, maybe – as well as her style of getting around… you know. Peter is grateful for all this, but I wish I could tell him more – even if I had one or two souvenirs, or photos. I have one photo – you've seen it – but nothing else. When they came to take me to the city, I didn't get a chance to pack my bag, if you know what I mean."

"What about your father?"

"No chance; he disappeared with some other family – or, maybe I should say other *tribe* – before I was five."

Then, he stopped and pointed out to the street. "Look, John," he said, "isn't that Paddy? There, up there, going up toward the uni?"

It was indeed our old boozing buddy, Paddy Two-Sticks. But something else struck me hard. "Saul, how'd you see him? I mean, how did you recognize him? He must be fifty yards away. Your sight's getting better."

Saul looked at me, poleaxed. "You're right! Jesus, how strange that I did not notice that. It must be happening very slowly… very gradually."

When he strolled out of Bernini's ahead of me, I noticed that he had no obvious limp. Another great change – if it was true.

I tapped him on the shoulder. "Listen, Saul, sorry about those nightmares, but they'll go away. And, look: you can walk! You can see! Is it a miracle?"

"You mean like in the Bible? Then who is doing the healing?"

"Well, I can't quote chapter and verse on this, but I recall a statement which the gospel-writer kept repeating: *'He went around making the blind see and the lame walk.'*"

"Something's going on, John, definitely. Maybe I should get myself down to Solway…"

19

Jane called me on the Friday.

"Hello, dearest John. How are you? I was just listening to a song by the late, great Warren Zevon. You know him? It's called "The Envoi" and it has lyrics like: *'Whenever there's a crisis, the president sends his envoi in.'* It's such a neat word. John, you are my envoi. You've been such a great help to us. Nothing's ever too much for you, and you ask so little in return. I was thinking of you all on your own so much; Patricia is still in Florida, isn't she? Well, listen, if you've got nothing arranged, please come over to me for lunch on Sunday. It'll be just you and me; cosy. Come at twelve-thirty and be on time."

On Saturday, my phone rang again – a number I did not recognize. It was Saul, calling from the phone in Jocky's flat.

"Guess what? Jocky phoned. He's coming back home, a week from Wednesday. He expects to arrive early, so would I mind vacating the flat by the previous Tuesday, at the latest? And, would I see that the place is clean and tidy? And, would I lock the door when I leave and put the keys through the letterbox? So, John, this opportunity coming up on Monday is now quite important."

"How's that? Are you going to tell me any more about it?"

"No, I can't, because I don't know. But, my point is the job includes accommodation. Could be just what I need to get settled a little."

"Okay, then all the best; give it all you have. Will I call you, to find out how it went?"

"No, I'll phone you. I don't mind phoning when it's a real one, like the phone I'm using right now – you know, one with a cord and a handpiece and a dial. That's a phone. No offence, John, but that gizmo you and everybody else are so in love with, it's not for me."

"Okay, I'll expect to hear from you on Monday."

Still wary and suspicious, I thought I could use the visit to Jane to find out more about this new job Saul was hoping for.

I did get information, but it was not quite on the subject I expected, when I mentioned to Jane that Jocky would be home in ten days, and Saul needed to be out by then.

Jane's eyes narrowed. "Jocky? Oh, dear; these days, I don't realize how time flies. Jocky's in jail in Barlinnie; got sixty days for common assault and breach of the peace – the usual Glasgow charges. I knew Jocky's mother; she was just as bad, although at least she did have some style – panache, you know? Like using a cigarette holder to smoke a Lucky Strike. Ridiculous. You should tell Saul to be well out of the way before Jocky arrives; he's a sociopath."

Then she added: "But at least he's not as bad as his brother Benny; now there is a real sick psycho, the kind who should never be allowed to mix with people."

"Benny?" No more could this be a coincidence than any of the rest, even if Benny is a fairly common name in Glasgow.

She explained that Peter had gone into town to do some browsing, and Mandor was visiting some old friends. She mentioned that she had really been impressed by my kindness and my demeanour, when I had visited her in the hospital. She also brought up the topic of Peter's health, and her worries about all the travelling.

"He's no traveller – not like his brother. And even Saul does very little travelling now."

I could not tell from this how much Jane knew about the background to Saul's meetings days, when he was travelling non-stop. I just remarked that Saul had done a lot of years of travelling, when he was a boy.

"You've given me an idea, but I'll need to sleep on it for a while. Peter is more than welcome to stay here, but I know deep down he's not convinced it would work. They've talked over getting a flat in the city to share, but that would be worse than that T.V. series *The Odd Couple*, years ago. And, on that subject, I'm afraid the proposed double-act project is doomed, too; it's just too much to ask, really. Sad, but they're right to be realistic. There was only one Laurel and Hardy."

"Saul did mention something to me about a job interview tomorrow. You're being quite coy about that, Jane."

"Oh, it's very little. I suppose Saul has built up a fantasy picture of some career and a place thrown in. Oh, dear; he might be disappointed. George came up with a wee idea to help Saul, and I like to encourage that; George is not known for coming up with ideas of any kind. I suppose we'll all find out tomorrow."

And so we did. As promised, Saul called about five p.m. on the Monday.

"What a day, John! Funny, in some ways. No, actually in *every* way. What a day – boy, oh boy! You never know what's round the next corner."

"Are you actually going to tell me anything?"

"Ah, well, I gets there on time, checks that the street number is correct and go up a flight of steps, leading to some offices. At the top stands a lady – well, a woman – wearing one of those clinging, invisible dresses. And totally buxom! She was not letting me past.

"'Sorry,' I said, 'I'm here about the job.' She just blew smoke in my face. 'George sent me; I'm from George,' I stammered, finding it difficult to focus on her face.

"'I'm from Paradise,' she replied, 'but it's gonna cost you.'

"'Paradise, you say?'

"'Yes, but I got kicked out.'

"Then the door opens and an ugly little guy appears. He says something, possibly in Italian, to Miss Paradise, and she shimmies inside. 'You lookin' for something?' he asks me.

"'I'm here about the job,' I say, and he laughs.

"'You're the wrong size, the wrong age and the wrong sex. If you're spying or something, or up to no good, I'll send Sergio to dissect you. Understand? Now, good day.'

"Honest, that was it. They could have been filming a movie!

"So, I went down the steps and noticed that the number written on the note was not 43, but 43A. I looked around and saw it: a kiosk; one of those cramped little boxes dotted around the city centre, which sold papers and cigarettes, sweets and stuff, the size of a standard garden shed. Above the little window was the number 43A. I knew the worst then, but I went closer and said hello to the man inside.

"'Ah, hello. You from George?' he asked me.

"'Yes,' I admitted.

"'Ees a nice wee job. Bit boring, but you meet a lotta different people here. And it's warm, and regular pay. Obviously there's a few things you have to learn – about newspapers and things, delivery times and that – but you look like a clever guy; it'll be easy for you. When can you start?'

"Still, something in me persisted. 'Erm, George did mention something about accommodation. What does that consist of, exactly?'

"'What is accommodation?'

"'A house, a home, a flat, an apartment… to live in.'

"'Ay, yes, yes, we did have a nice single room, a coupla streets away, but it caught fire yesterday, so that's pure shit. Maybe we find you something else. You wanna start now? I could show you what goes on. I could give you an induction.'

"John, I just turned and started walking. He shouted a few things, the third of which was very unsavoury and uncomplimentary. But it is over – over before it started. I would like to have a few words with that George fella! But, more to the point, Jocky's coming home."

"You know where he's been?"

"I can guess; on the phone, he said he only was allowed two minutes."

The days ticked by, and things between Peter and Saul seemed to have stalled. Their comic act was in cold storage, and Peter was considering cutting back on his visits to Glasgow. Additionally, a state of homelessness was approaching Saul. I could see it all frittering away.

So, I gave Saul a ring and suggested that, while there was time, he really should go to Rockcliffe. I offered to drive him and Peter down. Peter had mentioned an interesting hotel in Rockcliffe; I could stay there for one night, or maybe two, depending on how things unfolded, then bring Saul back.

Agreement at last.

PART THREE

20

Thursday morning was like schoolboys setting off on their summer holiday. Jane and Dorman, and even a few neighbours, stood waving handkerchiefs to us as we set off, the boys in the back both lively and relaxed. Jane had filled some bags with provisions, deepening the sense of a safari.

"Now, behave, boys! Saul, remember what I told you!"

Peter looked at Saul with raised eyebrows, and Saul shrugged his shoulders. I saw this through the rear-view mirror, and felt a little sad for the double act that was never to be.

The M74 would have been the less complicated route, skirting Dumfries on the way. The M77 was thirty minutes longer, but after we got past Ayr and Girvan it took us cross-country, through small towns and villages, which built up a feel of the southwest. Also, it meant that we ran along closer to Galloway Forest Park. Peter informed us that the park was the only designated dark-sky site in Britain, and the dearth of electric light in the area meant you could see stars and constellations you'd never see from any other vantage.

Peter suggested we stop for a break at the town of New Galloway, as it gave a kind of taste of the lifestyle in the area. So we did, and had some tea in a little café. Saul was intrigued and wondered aloud, several times, where the backstreets led to, beyond the one long main street. We talked him out of any adventures.

Driving leisurely, with the window down, the air was sweet but not cloying. We were moving through freshness and fragrance, as we took in views of rolling farmland, moorland, mudflats, forests, lochs and, at last, the water and beaches of the Solway Firth, with the Irish Sea lying beyond to the south. We were having fun, trying to guess the names of song tracks being played on the car radio, when the modest signpost for Rockcliffe creaked its welcome from a tree branch.

The cottage has always enjoyed a more unjustly sentimental history than other sorts of dwellings, and Peter's fitted the mould. There were no roses around the doorframe, and no burbling brook running nearby; the birds were not chirping – at least when we arrived. The stone of its construction looked so sturdy that it seemed more of a miniature castle than a cottage. Inside was sharply clean and tidy: a snug open fire and rather odd figurines, standing around on little shelves and cupolas. A lovely, striking wood-carving of the Virgin Mary stood on a mantel above the doorway of the kitchen. I didn't see the bedrooms, since I was staying elsewhere in a hotel.

A shingle path twisted its way down to the beach and, as soon as we had deposited our bags, Saul insisted we go down onto the sand and paddle. He said he hadn't smelt saltwater for a lifetime, and loved it so much, how had he ever gone without it? He was getting quite high, with tears in his eyes, hugging Peter dangerously, punching me on the shoulder and then pretending to spar with me like a boxer. He was still Crazy Horse.

The beach here gently shelved into the water, and the sea was mild. We scuffed along through the little breakers, like three boys out looking for crabs. Peter gave us some info about the area and pointed over to a little island.

"That's known as Rough Island. Strange wee place. I don't see anybody visiting it much, though you can if you want; up along that road there's a causeway, out to the Rough Island. The sea covers it for five hours at high tide, so you need to get your visiting times right. There are oystercatchers nesting there in May and June, so no visiting is allowed then."

"I'm taking notes, brother," said Saul.

"Then, you may want to add to your notebook, brother, that both of the nearest pubs are up that same road a couple of miles, in Kippford. One's much better than the other, as I'm sure you'll find out in time."

I had taken an open booking at a local hotel called The Crow's Nest. It was mid-afternoon, and I had arranged for the brothers to come up to the hotel for dinner at seven. That suited perfectly; Saul said he could do with a nap.

Peter replied: "Thank God! That's a wonderful idea."

The day was still going well. I checked into the hotel and came down to look around. Feeling peckish, I thought I'd ask for a sandwich. There had been a girl at the desk ten minutes before, but she was now nowhere to be seen. I dinged the bell.

A tall, lanky man, very like Basil Fawlty, appeared and snapped: "Yes?"

"Hello. I'm a new guest: John. I'd like a sandwich, if that's possible."

"Of course it is, of course it is. What do you want on it? Cheese and tomato?"

"Cheese and tomato would be fine. And some tea."

"Tea as well, eh? Right, back in a mo'."

Ten seconds later, his head popped back around the door. "Mayonnaise?"

"If there's any."

I sat down on a nice old couch and waited. Shortly, Basil came in with a tray and put it down on the table. "A pleasure," he said.

I looked down to see there were two small sandwiches of sliced tomato, and two small sandwiches of sliced cheese; they were separate. Beside them was a little dish with a weird spoon standing upright, in the thickest mayonnaise this side of the Nile delta. But I was hungry and it was tasty. The tea was marvellous, too. I then took a ramble outside.

I guessed it to be a Victorian building. However, squat and heavy at the east wing was a square stone tower, with crenelated ramparts, so maybe the place had an interesting history. The gardens were well stocked, but none of the colours gave off any glare. And, in the air hung that same sweet ambience I had sensed earlier, utterly unlike the city.

I went back in and saw on the door the notice: *"Proprietor: Harold Bone O.B.E."* I deduced that he must be Basil Fawlty, the sandwich-bearer. And, sure enough, there he stood at the desk, looking at me a little kindlier. We got to chatting.

I explained the circumstances of my visit, and was glad to hear that he was acquainted with Peter.

"Yes, yes, of course; comes in here now and again. Likes a little warm water in his brandy. Yes, a little peculiar – oh, sorry, I mean no disrespect; I love peculiar people. They are good for the hotel, for one thing; can give the place a bit of character. Guests seem to like character; not enough of it around these days. Although, this place is abounding in character and interest. Did you know, for example, that Black Archibald, the son of the famous Black Douglas, lived here in the mid-fourteenth century? Just like yesterday to some Gallovidians! You're not a Gallovidian, of course; they rarely come back once they've departed. I think, though, that your chap Peter is a Gallovidian… And he's come back, so perhaps I am talking snorkers." This was all delivered in almost one breath.

He inhaled and continued: "I don't know how long you'll be staying; I see you've left it open. That's fine – simply fine. If you do stay awhile, no doubt you'll want to visit Galloway Forest Park. It's just up the road from here, and I've heard it is the largest remaining wilderness in Britain. Not a man for wildernesses myself, I should add, but I have met people who are: forest junkies, you might say; can't get enough of deep, green silences, spooky noises in the treetops and unworldly sounds from unseen throats. Too spooky for me.

"Anyway, sorry, have to go: Isabel."

21

As I showered, I wondered if Peter had deliberately held back his knowledge of Mr. Bone, to increase the impact on me.

At 6.30, I was drinking some beer in the lounge, and no sign of Harold. There was a new face at the bar: a girl with very short hair. *Bit like Sinead O'Connor,* I thought. Then I felt a chill. So like Sinead O'Connor, in fact, I got a terrible foreboding about another doppelganger! But, no need to fear: the bar girl started to sing, and she sounded like an old crow.

My pals arrived at quarter to seven. In the dining room, several tables were occupied.

Ours was served by a young Mexican, who promised to play the Mexican guitar for us next time we came – but only if Senor Bone was away. "Meester Bone does not like Mexican music of any kind." He was a pleasant lad, and he told us rather proudly that people called him Banjo, which may have been his idea of a good P.R. stunt.

We ate local food for all courses, and it was superb – and astonishingly inexpensive. Peter threw in some local trivia from time to time. One surprising piece of info was that there existed still, since 1798, a Galloway Association of Glasgow, exclusive to Gallovidians who had moved residence to Glasgow. Peter had never followed up on this knowledge, and had no idea what kinds of stuff this Association might discuss or get up to; they could well have been mistaken for a local lodge of the Masons.

They spoke more and more about their parents. Obviously, Peter's knowledge was practically nil, and Saul's memory of his boyhood had never been very productive. He said that not only had his nightmares ceased, but he was beginning to have dreams about the past, and his days travelling around the south. Only fragments emerged from these dreams, but Saul hoped they might expand. And he had more to say:

"Being down here is better than any dreams, no matter how real they seem. Peter took me today to see the house where we were both born. It's still standing, though there is no farm now attached. Of course, the people living in it now would likely not know us, so we just had a look. But I did feel something. While we were there, Peter was asking me about our father, the Romany, and what he was like. It was so hard to think; the group we travelled in were organized quite differently from how city folk live. The man who I think was my father was – and I don't usually use such words – a beautiful man: beautiful to look at, to listen to and to be with. Also a calm man, which I think is rare among travellers; they are often up in arms about some grievance or other – most often their unjust treatment, and so on. But my father was a peacemaker; I have no memory of him ever quarrelling with my mother, even once. I was very young, but I think from the start I intuited why my mother needed to be with him – even though it meant running away from home, taking me and leaving baby Peter.

"And, Peter, can I take this moment to say something on that? I suppose our mother had to choose, and what a difficult choice it must have been. But maybe she thought life on the road with the Romanies would be just a little less tough on a one-year-old than on a newborn infant – so, you had to stay and I had to leave. We'll never know what she would think of us now: would she be pleased; proud? Maybe of you; you've made something of your life, against the most horrific obstacles and turns of bad luck: the death of your only son, the mutilation that ended your career, a failed marriage… But I was looking around your lovely cottage and thinking what a complete mess I have made of my life. I've been chasing phantoms all these years, content to have a roaring-boy reputation among riff-raff, and worse. Meanwhile, you have quietly progressed – and I bet we've yet to hear about the many other good deeds you've carried out. I've learned nothing.

"Well, maybe one thing, which I can pass on to you as advice; I ask you here and now: never go to a psychiatrist, because he'll drive you mad, digging into your mind. He'll lay before you all sorts of loathsome stuff, and tell you that this is you. It will lead to your mental collapse. I've been there. Neither of you know anything about this, but I've been at the point where the brain goes mushy and, worst of all, you know exactly what's happening."

This long, earnest speech moved Peter and me. Peter assured Saul, now a little emotional and in tears, that he had no plans or intentions to go near any psychiatrists. Why would he? He had friends to talk to, and he had a brother returned to him.

Saul was reassured and his spirits recovered quickly. Able to get back on the topic, he explained that Romany families seemed to operate within wider ties, with greater inter-relation than us. He explained how it would not be unusual, or remarked upon, for some man in the group, other than his father, to scold him, correct him or teach him some new skill. He just knew his father was there with him, and his support was absolute. As for his mother, of course, there was no ambiguity; in all her wildness and passion, her love and care for him never sagged.

Saul believed that she saw how her devotion to Saul's father could leave her son's life with a very stunted future. When she told him it was time for them to part, he was able to accept it with a strength which must have gone underground in him and remained, through his later life, the bedrock of his survival. His boyhood had been hard, rather than bucolic, and he had seen much of life in the raw, among people who had their share of rogues and villains living among them; many of the male travellers were the complete opposite to Saul's father, the peacemaker.

The three of us were in that pleasant and floating state of bliss which follows a fine meal, in warm company, when Peter started on an old song, "Tom Dooley", which we all knew from long ago. We joined along with him in parts, for it was a catchy melody with easy harmonies.

We were sort of in full cry, but sotto voce, when in came Mr. Bone, clanking across the room between patrons (some of whom had been showing signs of appreciation of our singing), like a creature of H.G. Wells. He paused at one table, where a gent spoke to him, and he beamed. Then he came over to us, to announce that he knew a new musical entertainment act for the hotel when he heard one! When could we sign up?

Saul, being a little tired and emotional, was confused, wondering who this long string of insanity was. But Bone put him at ease right away.

"So, you're Saul? Now, that is something. Do you know, Saul, you are the first ever Saul to stay at this hotel in my long time here? It is a great honour to greet the Great Saul. I look forward later to hearing some of your tales and exploits. Back soon."

And then he shot off through to the back, pausing for a moment to call back over his shoulder: "I'll keep the bar in the back room open 'til after midnight. Anybody who fancies a cosy snifter is welcome to join me."

When I look back and try to pinpoint the deciding moment, the turning of the tide, it may have been then. The three of us sat deep in chairs, around a long, low table of oak, along with Bone and four other hotel guests; two couples: one in their thirties and the other for whom time had run out, who both seemed older than walnuts.

When Harold (as he now wished to be known) served our drinks, he joined us, and the talk ran quite smoothly. The male walnut, in a deceptively light and pleasant voice, started telling us something of the lore of the area – some historical, some legendary – and some strange stuff about the local fauna, especially the horses. Walnut Ted insisted that there were still herds of Galloway horses which could be found nowhere else on the planet, and no scientist knew why. His wife, Tulip, warned him jokingly not to get started on any stories about headless horses.

"That's perfectly alright, Tulip, my sweet," he said: "the stories are actually about headless horsemen, my dear. Galloway isn't the Bronx."

Karen and Bobby, the younger couple, chuckled along at us old flower-power hippies, enjoying the banter which seemed very much a novelty to them. Perhaps they came from a place where you were not supposed to be witty or amusing after you passed thirty.

Karen introduced the subject of the travellers and border gypsies, and enquired whether any could still be seen or met. Harold knew of a travellers' resting spot at Thistle Grove, near Dumfries, which had about twelve sites; the only other one he knew was way over near Stranraer. Bobby hoped their use of the term "gypsy" wasn't offensive, but Harold thought that intermarriage over the years between the two groups had blurred any distinction between them. Peter had been quiet for a bit, but now began to talk quite feelingly about the travellers, their life and their never-ending conflict with settled communities. He insisted, having met a lot of them, that they were far from the stereotype of shiftless and irrational no-gooders; they were proper nomads of the world.

I learned that they are committed to the ideology and practices of nomads. In ancient times, the first nomads were hunters, who moved around in search of food. Then there were pastoral nomads. And today, in built-up countries, there are what you might call "tinker" nomads, although the word tinker has nearly always an offensive implication. They seem able to create a sort of landscape of memories, which helps them to keep returning to the places they treasure. What I learned, really, was that travelling is a state of mind.

Ted's view was that, like most other social groups, they contain members who let the side down, time after time, sometimes disgracing themselves, and the reputation and status of their kindred. He had seen a lot of squalor and deprivation, like in many over-run cities, which left the image of the romantic gypsy life a faded dream, at best. He knew of initiatives that governments and local councils would come up with, every so often, issuing recommendations after three years of study – usually the same ones as twenty years before, often to do with health and education.

So went the discussion, a little clichéd at times, though maybe each of us learnt a little in the course of the chat.

I felt it was time to change the subject, when Saul spoke up:

"Up in Glasgow, where I am just now, 'gypsy' is a term of abuse. You probably know that. My brother Peter lives down in these parts. Like me, he was born right here, but he was prevented from the opportunity to live the travelling life; he's never been a gypsy. But I am a gypsy. My mother was from the settled community here, but she took me and joined a gypsy caravan, to be with my father – and Peter's, of course; the first ten years of my life were spent on the road.

"I've been going through some changes recently, and in this sort of upheaval of the mind I've been having, things from those days are starting to come back to me. For example, like most kids I was a bit scruffy. There was a village near here – I just cannot recall the name – but each time we came to visit it, maybe twice a year or so, I was scrubbed thoroughly. My hair was given special attention with… I don't know what: some oils and lotions, until I looked like an oversized pixie, or a creature from the forest. The women would give me a basket with little bunches of fresh flowers, and I would have the task of going around this village, on my own, to sell them; there was nothing else in the basket. The villagers loved it and they loved me. Some of the loveliest girls I fell in love with were the daughters of that place, and when I got back to the wagons (the flowers all sold – always), the basketful of money I upended drew great cries of joy. I was not told beforehand the names of the flowers I carried, and this was deliberate, because among my folk I was known for making up strange names for things, spontaneously. This I would do when a village lady would ask: 'And, what are those crimson ones, my dear?'

"'Them's baboukles,' I'd said; 'autumnly baboukles. You mustn't eat them.' How they laughed!

"'But it's not autumn,' she'd reply.

"'They're very early autumnly baboukles.'"

The company was now in fine form, and so it stayed, well into the night. Maybe Harold Bone never slept; he was still standing there, washing glasses at the bar, when we all trooped out, promising one another eternal fealty and dedication, planning what great times we had still to share, and all that. When I reached my room and opened the window a little, I could still hear two voices strangling some song, on their way down to the cottages.

22

The next day's plan was for an early lunch at the cottage, then a little tour of some of the huge forest. I had time for egg and toast in the hotel before leaving. Just as well I had no more, because when I arrived about noon a lovely smell told me some fine fish was frying. I joined Peter and Saul at the dining table. From the kitchen beyond came the merry sizzle and crackle of cooking.

"That's okay, John," Peter said; "all taken care of. Have some of that good tea."

In from the kitchen came Pearl, carrying plates of fish, salad and fresh bread on a big tray; there were four plates of food. She joined us as we ate.

"I thought you were doing the cooking, Peter."

"No, no, John; I only catch them. Pearl transforms them from those slippery creatures with staring eyes into what you see before you."

"You caught them?"

"I caught two large bass this morning – about six pounds worth. You won't get better, John."

Of course, I thought to myself: *Peter the Fisherman.* How could I have missed it?

Pearl, like many women of these parts, was skilled in filleting and preparing all sorts of sea life. Bass was for her a very simple challenge. Just taste and you'd see.

Our talk moved from food to city life, and Pearl had a lot of questions; it was clear that she was curious about the attractions of a big city.

"I was always a big film fan and I loved the cinema – the whole experience of it: the huge, dark hall; a screen vastly bigger than any T.V.; the real sense of being removed from your day-to-day life. Of course, we see films on T.V. – as many as you like – but going to the pictures is in my D.N.A. I also love the big churches, the styles and the way they were built. I know Glasgow isn't Rome or Paris, but some of the things I've learned are quite fascinating. Of course, I can travel up now and again, and Peter has been kind enough to take me twice – that time at Jane's we had a great day… Anyway, we are where we are."

Peter brought the talk to the day's itinerary. We could get from Rockcliffe to the Galloway Park Visitor Centre – a place with the name Clatteringshaws – in under an hour.

So, in true Scottish macho style, we left Pearl with a sinkload of dishes to wash and toodled off, like some scene from *Wind in the Willows*, the back tyres sending dust up from the gravel. It was a glorious drive into new terrain. The Visitor Centre was our target, so we headed straight there, and agreed to do any stopping and exploring on the way back.

The centre was abuzz, with all the usual folk on late summer outings and holidays. It is positioned by a lake, and there are water activities galore. The centre is close to the dark sky-site and, at night, from anywhere around here appears the most overwhelming vision of the heavenly bodies. It was fully booked out, of course, but we were told the spectacle is even greater one month from then.

We took a walk through the forest, good, neat paths and signposts everywhere; oak, sycamore, pine and yew all quietly watching us, as they do. We drove and stopped again at a layby, where a clearing in the woods opened before us, a welcoming glade with soft, lighter greens all around. Saul was affected, and said it struck him as being like a song he had heard long ago, where there was a line he now recalled. Not only that, but he made a faltering stab at singing the tune:

"There was open ground, where a man could linger
for a week or two, for time was not our master,
then away you'd jog, with your horse and dog,
nice and easy; no need to go faster."

Moments like this were profound for all three of us. They were brothers, but they never made me feel like an outsider at any time.

As we watched and listened to the birdsong, Saul asked: "How long do birds live for? I mean, do they live a long time?"

Peter said that he knew parrots and macaws lived for thirty or forty years. From what he'd gathered, birds which got past the chick stage usually then had at least two to three years.

At this point, as we slowed, a man coming up to pass us remarked: "Couldn't help hearing your discussion. Life span of birds is an interesting subject; in nearly every species you get a solid average, but always with numerous exceptions. Many crows live into their twenties; they're the ones to watch – I mean watch out for, not just watch. Crows are as clever as dolphins; take in a crow and you'll soon be homeless! Kingfishers are safer… and more beautiful. I do believe sometimes that angels take the shape of kingfishers.

"Anyway, I'll leave you with that thought; I have miles to go before I sleep, as somebody once put it. Ha-ha!"

Saul's response was: "We place far too much importance on cities, don't we? And, for what? Money, I suppose. Out here, you can be in a different life – no question."

We drove on again, and stopped for some coffee at a wayside tearoom. The branches of the trees across the road were fantastical in their writhing, and very distinctive. So much so that Saul told us, almost in a whisper, that he recognized these trees from long ago.

"I mean those actual trees over there. This must have been near one of our stopping places. We had stopped, and I wandered off into the woods; I came into a clearing behind those trees. From the other side emerged a girl of about my own age: nine or ten; she had grasses and weeds tangled in her hair – she was even weirder than the tree branches. She stopped and looked at me, boldly and piercingly, from twenty feet away. Then, her arm went back and, next thing I knew, I was struck on the face, just below the eye, by a piece of flint. I bent and picked it up, and when I straightened up she was out of sight, her crazy laughter fading into the undergrowth. I wanted so much to talk to her, and felt a sharp pain in my chest when I realized she was gone. I still have a little scar right here. My mother only said: 'You'll have to be more careful. That girl you met was "The Mad Girl".' I nodded, knowing that if she was mad, then so was I."

As he got to the end of the little story, Saul came back to us from wherever he had been. It was like patiently watching, as a man very slowly came out of a deep coma. Saul's memory cells were being gently revived, and there could be little doubt that being in this place with his brother had nurtured that new growth.

Just as we arrived back at the cottage, around five, a call from my agent reminded me of an important appointment the following midday. I decided to travel back the same evening and rest up at home, before what might be an important meeting with an impatient publisher. Peter, Saul and I talked it through.

Saul was not ready to return yet, so he was staying on, to Peter's delight. And Pearl's, for that matter; she had seen through the bracken and shrubbery, to some more agreeable meadow, farther inside Saul. They insisted that they would not call on my help for any further transporting.

As a memento of my short stay in Galloway, Peter had wrapped for me what he said was a little work of local art, which would be good for my room. Driving home to Glasgow alone was quite relaxing, but I wished I had the brothers with me.

23

Back in Glasgow, I caught up on some business. I actually did some writing work, agreed new deadlines, and by teatime on the Saturday I felt ready for a nice drink of beer. I wasn't ready yet for The Palace, so I scooted down to The Comedians, where there might be a little live music.

I met up with Matty Brennan there and we got nattering. I was just starting to tell him about the glories of Galloway, when my phone rang. It was Jane.

"Hello, sweetums. Got a call from Peter today; so happy! Him, too – and Saul. Boy, this is all so marvellous! A family has come back from the dead, and you, John, have been Merlin the Wizard!"

"Did Merlin do that kind of thing? Bring back folk from the dead?"

"Of course. Anyway, listen, you sceptic; I have something quite exciting to say, but I am also sworn to a surprise – a surprise for you! Unfortunately, it will entail you going back down to Rockcliffe. Oh, dear, I know they promised they wouldn't ask again, but it's me asking, John: me, the prize-winning rose of yesteryear. Can you do it, John?"

"If I am available, of course I will, no problem. They are great company, the Terry lads; we had such fun together. When do they want me to go?"

"Actually, it can be any day next week, Monday to Friday, I understand. Saul does not seem to be missing his old haunts yet, so you take your pick and I'll pass on the word."

"Make it Tuesday. And tell them I don't want any emotional partings; no sloppy stuff."

"Yes, Master."

I guessed the surprise was for my birthday, which fell on the Wednesday of the following week. How they would know that was puzzling, but Jane, with her Boy Wonder Dorman, seemed good at finding out hidden matters.

Later, I sat for a while and revisited some of the outstanding moments of the previous few days. Only then I remembered that Peter had given me a parting gift. I found my bag and unwrapped the little wood-carving; very dark, reddish wood had been chiselled and shaped into an animal of some kind – hard to say what, but probably of the cat family; it was standing still but very tense, head looking toward the left. I was a little flummoxed, but very impressed by the wooden object I was holding; the way the various tensions and stretching had been captured was amazing. The creature stood on a simple plinth of some other kind of wood. It required a place of honour, so I found a spot for it in the middle alcove of my Spanish dresser. Perfect. Must find out more info from Peter. I got excited at the thought of another little jaunt to Rockcliffe.

On Monday night, Peter phoned.

"Everything in order, John?"

"You bet. When do you want me?"

"Well, at first we thought as early as you can conveniently make it: maybe about noon. But that's two drives in the same day, so why don't you come down a little later, maybe for around four, and stay over, to be fresh for the return on Wednesday morning?"

On Tuesday at 2.30, I had reached the top end of the forest. *Better slow down,* I thought; *I'm early.*

I stopped at a café named Green Glade and listened to some Josh Ritter; great new album. That let me arrive just on four. There were Laurel and Hardy, standing by the gate.

Saul got straight to the main matter: "Did Jane mention a surprise?"

"I can't remember," I lied; "if so, I have forgotten it. Is it a good or a bad surprise?"

"God, God, good, good! Come on in and we'll tell you all about it."

This was not sounding like a birthday present – and so it turned out.

Saul was bouncing, as in the bad old days, but this time he was on a safer propellant. His eyes were glowing.

"John, all last Friday we were head-to-head on all this, as deep in thought as you can imagine. We had a lot of details to think about, as you'll hear in a minute, but we came to a big agreement. You ready, John?"

He could hardly have lengthened the build-up any further; it was too much.

"John, when you go back in the morning to the city, you're not taking me – I'm not coming back there – but you are taking Peter; he is going there. From the minute I got here, a spell started to weave around me. If the spell has imprisoned me, I don't care; this is where I belong. This is the world Saul the boy lived in, and was nourished in; this is what made me. After I left here, a lot of things tried to unmake me, and a lot of those forces succeeded. I lost my whole identity. Remember the doppelganger? I see now that I was chasing *myself* down Great Western Road, trying to find my own identity.

"Peter has helped me to understand this. But, not only that; Peter is a quite different character from me. He has the inner strength to live life anywhere, wherever he finds himself. Do you want to explain to John, Peter?"

"Sure. Forget inner strength; I just had to keep going. Down here, with few distractions, I could concentrate on surviving the trials I was set. It's a lovely part of the world and it has been right for me, but there are things in the city that I miss; interests I would love to pursue. The thought just came to me: maybe I should finally go to the city to stay. And, of course, the corollary followed: Saul should come down here and stay."

I was taken aback, and I could not speak for a moment. Could Saul possibly survive down here? And yet, I saw how sweetly tempting it could be.

Peter had obviously started to get the project moving; "Jane has so many contacts that she already has two apartments for me to look at. I have been in touch with several people, about reorganizing the ownership and entitlements to the cottage, and so on. I am convinced that, although this could not be more unlike Glasgow, Saul will thrive down here."

"You bet, John! And, guess what else, John? That brother of mine is scared I'm gonna steal his woman! Yes, he is. So, Pearl is going along with Peter; I'm kicking the two of them out and amalgamating the two cottages. Soon, I will expand and become the Lord of Rockcliffe!"

Peter became theatrical: "Tonight, we hold a solemn supper, sir… Fail not our feast!"

I did not fancy the part of Banquo one little bit, but bowed and said humbly: "My lord, I will not."

The supper was anything but solemn. It began at 7.30 in The Crow's Nest, where we had laughed and sang one week before.

"Wouldn't it be splendid," said Harold, "if we could have a weekly date like this, to carouse and sup and sing?"

"Indeed, Harold," I agreed. "All delights eventually lose their salt, even Saul Terry, but let's enjoy it while it's here."

"I love the style you chaps have when you talk – well up to the high traditions of The Crow's Nest. But now I must put on my kitchen vestments and give some help to my minions."

The dining room was a little busier. Some people from Japan got into a hilarious mix-up with Harold, about the kind of chopsticks they were hoping for. I felt like calling over, "Just don't order the sandwiches," but realized how much extra uproar that would cause.

The evening was taken up with the future changes, the hopes and worries attached to them, and a shared sense of new adventures beginning. Last time, our focus had been on the past; now it had switched.

An idea had been nagging at me and, before the dessert arrived, I mentioned it: "Saul, there's one thing I haven't heard you speak about. This is a big, big region, much bigger than a city; how are you going to get around? Because I know that if you don't get moving around, your sky will turn very cloudy; an attack of cabin fever could bring down this whole enterprise."

"You're right, John. My good brother Peter suggested we don't make much of this, but I have to: Peter is buying me a car, second-hand – a Nissan Note, nice for nipping around these parts. So kind of him. It's part of the agreement and decisions we took the other day. Isn't he a champ? Oh, and by the way, John, let me apologize for dragging you back down here. We could have told you on the phone, but hated that idea. Phones – I hate them! They can't handle a moment like this. At least again you'll get a wee rest from our yapping, on the drive back."

"You didn't do any dragging, Saul, but I will admit that I am glad and relieved you have got a car again. Well done, Peter – and Saul, don't wreck it! And no tickets; you're too old for a horse now."

"Saul, you'll be in heaven down here. Already he's made friends and got people talking. And there's more, but I was asked by Harold to wait 'til he gets a moment to join us."

That moment did not come until we were once more ritually

welcomed into the back bar. At first, it was only ourselves.

Harold asked Peter: "Well, what did he think of it?"

"I don't know. John, did you like the gift?"

"Oh, heavens, so rude of me! I've been so caught up in all this new stuff I forgot to thank you. It is an amazing artefact; I love it. Actually, I don't know what creature it represents, but it doesn't matter; it guards my castle, night and day."

Harold laughed. "Brilliant! It's the Last Panther – or, rather, the last carving of the Last Panther. A hundred years ago, a large family of black panthers roamed the western Borders. They dwindled into extinction, but someone got one great photo of what was probably the last of the pack – then one of our carvers made the carving Peter gave to you."

"What do you mean, one of your carvers?"

Peter and Saul were smiling, and were obviously already in the know.

"The tower at the northeast corner of the building lay unused for a long time. Then it was tried as a gym, then as a place of worship by some Pagan sect; I think it also had a spell as a chess club, but it can be a long way to come, just to get beaten at a game of chess. So, it has been lying empty. Then one day, about two years ago, two men and two women appeared at my door; I could see they weren't looking for bed and breakfast. In fact, they were travellers, from the site about eight miles from Dalbeattie. They had heard about the tower, knew it wasn't being used, and asked straight out if they might rent it once a week, purely for one purpose: to make their wood carvings. Fond as I am of you chaps,

I am no great pal of the travellers; I've seen both sides to them. But, I knew that if I said something such as I would make some enquiries, look into it and get back to them – you know, the usual rejection by delay – then they would walk away. So, instead I said: 'Come and have a look at the place, and tell me more about these carvings.' One of them, named Barnabas, had a cloth bag, and took out a few samples; they were captivating. Tinkers have always been associated with making and selling wooden clothes-pegs, but these were in a different world; the close detail and grasp of just where a line should go and stop… Dogs, monkeys, fish, crocodiles and people, too; a few little houses… tremendous skill was in this work. Anyway, we came to an agreement: they could use the Tower on Thursdays, from six 'til eleven, provided that, if any locals showed an interest in learning the craft and working with them, they would permit that. They loved the idea. Most Thursdays now there are between twelve and sixteen people!

"We just call them carvers; it's more mystical, working away and learning an ancient skill. And, John, guess what? Saul is joining on Thursday."

Saul grinned and almost blushed, but that scarcely slowed down the rattle of Harold, as he went careering through his narration:

"I showed Saul a couple of carvings, and he was telling me of his days working in the sawmill – surely the two trades are distant cousins. Our plan is to introduce Saul as the 'Keeper of the Carvings'; he'll keep them safe, be in overall charge of the meetings, and help organize into some shape what can be a real guddle at times. Barney and his folk accept this, so I am hoping to put Saul on a wage, as a specialist employee of the hotel. I will work towards getting some grants from the council, because this could be a boost to tourism, as well as a bridge between the different communities."

At this point, Saul got in quickly enough to interrupt the flow of Bone: "I did like that job in the sawmill; learned quite a bit about woods: hard, soft, fruit, the importance of the grain... I loved the smell of the timber and, even more, of the sawdust: big, fresh heaps of it – intoxicating sometimes, depending on the particular tree. Yes, I loved it."

"Did you stay there long?"

"Nah, at the time I was starting to do quite well playing the bagpipes: won a couple of medals and told myself I was a future star, born to be a great piper. So, I gave up the sawmill. Of course, the rise to fame and glory did not materialize, and I had to be content with earning a bit of money playing at weddings, Burns suppers, of course, funerals and birthdays. I was self-employed, as they say – and that was the trouble: I needed somebody above me, to keep my mind on the job; it suits me better to be working for a boss. All that was long ago, but I am looking forward to getting among wood again, learning the craft from these masters of the art."

Harold came back with a complimentary bottle of Champagne for us; the Flag of Hope was flying. A toast was proposed, but before we raised our glasses, Saul asked:

"Was The Tower ever used for entertainment: music, plays, variety shows…?"

"Off and on it has been, sometimes for special occasions, but I don't think there was ever a resident act or group. It has good acoustics, too."

"Then there would have been our chance as a comedy double act! My aunt had a brainwave that we should call them 'Saul and Pepper', but nobody laughed. But now I have seen the real idea, the real breakthrough; I'm serious now. I've thought this right through from olden times, and I'm convinced the double act which never got started should have been called simply 'Peter and Paul'. You, brother, can still be Peter, but from now on I'm going to be Paul, not Saul! And not even as a part of any double-act; just Paul, the brother of Peter. 'The Two Terries'."

Harold remarked that he had read somewhere about someone else, who had done that very same thing. "Can't exactly remember whether it all went smoothly for him after that, though."

With that, he asked us to raise our glasses: "To Peter and Paul!"

24

Next morning, Peter wanted to show Paul a few tips about catching fish. So, I told them I'd be off, and leave them to it while the tide was right.

From my car, I called out: "When shall we three meet again?" It was very crummy, but I said it to hide my emotions.

As I drove slowly up the street, I saw in my mirror that Pearl had come to stand between them, arms around their waists. Was it just sentimental tosh? It felt like more than that.

Peter had said that he would get in touch, and we would soon meet in the city. Paul had made no such promises.

"I am going to build a new life here – or maybe pick up some strands of the old life I left, many years ago. I'm going to be too busy for meetings, dinners and the like. I've got a mobile phone, as you well know, and there is also a landline phone in the cottage, so don't worry; you can find me at any time. Of course, we'll have great fun in the months ahead. But now I hear the city calling you."

Over the following month, I was in regular touch with Peter and Pearl. I visited them several times in their new flat, quite close to the Clyde, and lent a hand with a few chores. Jane and Dorman were there on one occasion, but not George or Jean, so I probably wouldn't find out the real story behind the ghastly wild-goose chase George had sent Saul on, over to Cardonald. But, for five weeks there was not a sound from Saul (I could not yet get used to "Paul").

One day, when things were quiet and off the boil, Peter surprised me. He phoned and said: "Isn't it time I paid a visit to this illustrious tavern, which has meant so much to you and Paul? The Palace of Mirrors, right? When are you going to give me the tour? What about tomorrow lunchtime?"

I went over to pick Peter up. He was alone; no Jane; no Dorman. "They're at a meeting, I think."

"Right, let's go."

And off we went, along the Great Western Road.

We stopped on the pavement for a minute, to get a look at the front of the pub, with its inscriptions.

"Do you ever listen to Bob Dylan?" asked Peter then, to my surprise.

"I do, yes; I've listened to some of his work."

"And?"

I shrugged. I had the feeling of revisiting some question from the past.

"No matter. Let's have a look inside."

As Peter strolled around inside, talking to himself a little, I suddenly saw a deep likeness of his brother in him. He sat down and decided he'd have a shandy.

"Must toughen up my drinking, if I'm to be at home in

Glasgow, eh, John?"

"It depends on when you come in. In the morning, breakfasts are served and you get an older, quieter clientele. Then there's the afternoon crowd. Then there's the crazy gang, at night. I'm afraid Saul is a fully paid-up member of the crazy gang – or *was*."

At that moment, a shadow fell across the table. I looked up and there was Lydia, standing right behind Peter.

"Hello, John. Remember me? We were in a fight together."

"Of course I remember you, Lydia, even if we were all rather sloshed that night. Sometime in August, wasn't it?"

"I don't know. At least Saul is looking a bit more sober. How you been, Saul? Not going to say hello?" At this point, she was standing directly behind Peter, and she moved around and slid in beside us. Only then did she see her mistake.

"Oh, Jesus! Who's this? Who is this, John? Has something happened to Saul? He looks... I dunno... he's... Oh, wait a minute – you aren't Saul! You're his double, but you're not Saul. So, who are you?" By now, her anxiety was rising, and the bar-staff were alert, because Lydia had a record of bar-room instability.

"Calm down, Lydia, calm down; it was an easy mistake to make. This is a second cousin of Saul's. His name is Matthew; everybody calls him Matt. He lives in London and he's up visiting. Thought he might find Saul in here, but I've just been telling him he's come at the wrong time of day; Saul's a night-owl." I tried to give Peter's ankle a nudge under the table, as a warning, but Lydia was already looking very closely at us.

"Is he deaf and dumb, Cousin Matt?" she asked, sarcastically.

"Don't be silly, Lydia. I'm just explaining because a lot of people are making the same mistake as you just did. Matt, this is a friend of Saul; they go back quite a long way together."

"Very pleased to me you, my dear," spoke Peter, in his dark, rumbling voice. "My cousin has particularly good taste, I see."

"Is Saul coming in here to meet you? Because if he is not, I have an important message for him; I could ask you to pass it on."

"It's unlikely Saul will be in here today, Lydia, but I'd be glad to pass on any message."

"Tell him Lydia has got good news: Agnes is out of prison; the charges against her were suddenly dropped and they've let her go. But tell him Lydia has also got bad news: Jocky suspects that Agnes got out as part of a deal, in which she told the detectives a lot about Jocky and Sandy; they're now sweating… and waiting. They're unhappy with the person who recruited Agnes, and that was Saul. With the heat on them right now, I don't suppose they'll try anything, but Saul should be told."

"I'll pass on the news, good and bad. Thanks, Lydia."

"I'm not stopping. I've called in here a few times; now I'm glad I saw you and that's done. 'Bye, Matt. You should go back to London; there's too many bad people in Glasgow."

Peter waited until she had gone, then remarked: "I think my brother just got out of here in time, if that little encounter is anything to go by."

He looked around. "But I see what you mean: this pub does have some attractive features. If drinking in a pub is your thing, then this would be the kind of place to come to. But, as for the drinkers, that's different; it could be hard to stay out of harm's way. Though you seem to have managed it, John."

"I've been lucky. And, I have a policy of keeping things at arm's length and allowing no exceptions. Except maybe Saul."

On a Friday, near the end of October, among the usual bank and commercial mail, the postman pushed through the letterbox a white envelope, with my name and address handwritten on it – how old-fashioned it looked. I chucked the business mail aside and slit open the envelope, then sat down to read:

"My dear friends in Glasgow, my dear brother Peter and his lovely girl Pearl, my kind Aunt Jane and her servant Mandor, and my closest of friends and shotgun rider John,

"I write to let you know how things are progressing.

"Eventually I almost gave in to the easy option and called you on the phone. But I am no good on the phone; I get agitated and forget what I meant to say. It's too quick for me. So, I am setting down in writing such news as I think you might be interested in. I will send the letter by post to John, and ask him to convey any details to the rest of you.

"My first plan was to roll up the sleeves and rearrange everything in the cottage, so as to stamp my own personality on it. Then I saw how such thinking had been at the root of my foolish, wayward life. I moved nothing, I changed

nothing, and I started to learn how rewarding it is to put less before more.

"Down at the water, too, I started to learn. My first attempts at catching fish were laughable; the fish could more easily have caught me! But again, how strange: the more I let them come to me, rather than go after them, the more successful I was. But I never catch more than one or two. Catching fish is becoming easier, but preparing and filleting them is a different matter – why are they so dang slippery?

"My main business, as you might have guessed or hoped, has been in the Tower, with the carving folk. Some of them do not like being called carvers – I don't know why; maybe it has some bad connotations. In any case, we are a merry bunch, and I have noticed joyfully, over the weeks, that we are all now at home throwing insults at one another, and telling jokes which have no respect for authority or political correctness. I cannot yet claim to have made much progress with my woodcraft, though. In fact, I injured a finger quite badly with a sharp chisel, just three nights ago, but already it is mending. It has been a long time, maybe the first time ever, since I felt so much part of a group.

"Harold sends his best wishes to John and Peter. He says to tell you his life has been transformed since I came on the scene. Certainly there are more bookings at the hotel, and Harold has taken on a rather fearsome rhino of a woman, to be his assistant manager. But I found out that a

lot of the fearsomeness is just show, to impress Harold. She is a great bundle of fun and laughter, as Harold is sure to find out eventually.

"I see a lot of Harold throughout the week, and by evening I am usually pretty tired. So, I explained to him that I can no longer take part in those late-night sessions in the back bar; that decision has, in turn, made it easier for me to stop drinking alcohol altogether – much easier than I had feared. I have lots of sins to pay for, and who knows how little time.

"As winter approaches, there is more opportunity at night to sit and think. I found in the first few weeks that my thoughts kept running back to Glasgow, and the mayhem of the connections I had. I blindly made associations which put me in peril, and rasped along as if I was invincible. The news that Agnes has been set free is a great relief to me; I cried at the news. As to the bad side of that story, I spent a long time hiding in plain view from gangsters, and they left me alone, so I guess they will not bother pursuing me down here. At the same time, I will not be phoning Jocky to give him my new address, and I trust that none of you will either. If any of them do come knocking, they will have to make do with tea! And, trouble not, if they do ever come I will be ready.

"Peter was kind enough to leave behind many of his books for me, and my day usually ends in reading from his library. Just now I am enjoying a very strange book by

Mervyn Peake, called 'Titus Groan'. It is the most fantastic world I have ever entered, and I have been in a few. Even stranger, since I started reading Peake's book, I have had the best sleeps of my life, dreamless and unconfined.

"I have much more to tell you, especially about my travelling friends. I meet some of them on Thursday evenings, but I have also been up to their site a few times; I am building trust and affection between us. I have told them nothing of my birth and origins, yet I am sure some of them sense there is a strong bond between us. One of them, a lovely woman called Granwen, has offered to tell my fortune – that should be fun; who knows where it will lead me? Deep calls to deep.

"In my next letter, I hope to share with you a lot more detail about my travelling friends. That is where my future lies, I know. It is wonderful. A circle being completed.

"God bless you all,

"Paul."

I read the letter twice. As I was replacing it in its envelope, I noticed something printed in handwriting, on its back:

"The First Letter of Paul to The Glaswegians."

About the Author

James Bovill has lived and worked in the greater Glasgow area for most of his life. *Saul of Solway* is his fourth novel.

Acknowledgements

The publisher would like to thank Russell Spencer, Matt Vidler, Laura-Jayne Humphrey, Lianne Bailey-Woodward, Leonard West and Susan Woodard for their hard work and efforts in bringing this book to publication.

About the Publisher

L.R. Price Publications is dedicated to publishing books by unknown authors.

We use a mixture of both traditional and modern publishing options, to bring our authors' words to the wider world.

We print, publish, distribute and market books in a variety of formats including paper and hardback, electronic books, digital audiobooks and online.

If you are an author interested in getting your book published, or a book retailer interested in selling our books, please contact us.

www.lrpricepublications.com

L.R. Price Publications Ltd,
27 Old Gloucester Street,
London, WC1N 3AX.
020 3051 9572
publishing@lrprice.com

Printed in Great Britain
by Amazon